Aftermath

Cover Credits

Cover image by David Carr-Smith, from his study of improvised
architecture in the industrial squats of Amsterdam:
www.davecarrsmith.co.uk
Cover design by Laurie MacMillan, Sunfield Design:
www.sunfielddesign.com
Author photo by Judith M. Daniels:
www.judithmdaniels.com

Grassroots Press

ISBN: 1-4392-1076-4
ISBN-13: 978-1439210765
Library of Congress Control Number: 2008908443

Visit www.booksurge.com to order additional copies.

SCOTT CAMPBELL

AFTERMATH

2009

Aftermath

For Richard

PART I

H arry Garrett waits.

He stands at his two-story wall-to-wall window, hands clasped loosely behind his back, and stares out at the endless rush of people on the turnpike, hurrying from their homes to their jobs, from their jobs to their summer vacations, from their vacations back to their homes again, breathless, exhausted, hungry for more, gobbling up their lives, and he waits.

Harry hates this more than most anything. Maybe, he thinks, because it seems he's done little but wait for the past three years. Counting his footsteps, counting the stairs, humming the same annoying tune over and over again. But if he's honest with himself, he has to admit that in fact he has been waiting much of his life.

Sometimes he thinks it all goes back to that afternoon in his boyhood. It was a gloomy November day, that time of year when the entire world seems to be withdrawing. The birds had gone. The leaves had gone. The sun had retreated behind a permanent wall of gunmetal grey.

He was waiting for his mother to pick him up from his piano lesson in front of the Methodist Church where his teacher was music director. He'd had his lesson in the basement, where he usually sat uneasily on the fringes of weekly youth fellowship meetings, and afterwards his teacher had come out of the church with him, locking the door behind them, and hurried off down the street, turning to wave then turning back again to shoulder into the cold.

Harry shifted his weight from foot to foot, shifted his music from mitten-less hand to mitten-less hand, blowing hot breath on the other. A few half-hearted snowflakes drifted around him like lint. He looked up at the glowering sky, wishing that the sun would come out for just a moment to warm him, then he noticed the warm yellow light in the barbershop across the street.

He wondered if maybe he should wait there, to get out of the cold. There were people there, and fragrant powders, and steam hissing from the heating pipes. But what would he say when he walked in? Would they be mad if he didn't get a haircut? Would they laugh at him? They were laughing now; would he get the joke? Shy and awkward, watchful at ten, Harry decided maybe it would be better just to wait; his mother would be along, in time.

Hunching his shoulders in his too-big coat, he looked up at the sky again and in that moment, to his surprise, the clouds pulled apart and he was suddenly bathed in warmth and light. The light didn't cover the rest of the street, just the corner where Harry was standing, as if life itself had reached out to him and said *Harry. Here, have some.*

It's a parable that Harry has carried with him ever since, without entirely knowing it, like a secret talisman in his pocket—a vague but comforting assurance that if he's patient enough, if he just stands on the corner long enough, the skies will open up and offer themselves to him again, fulfilling the promise of all that life seems to hold just beyond his reach.

Harry sighs and pulls out a handkerchief to mop the sweat from his brow. The hottest July on record, he thinks, wondering if he's made it up or if he actually heard it somewhere. He stuffs the handkerchief back in his pocket and checks his watch again. Eleven forty-five. She is fifteen minutes late, as much time as you give a full professor: he is free to go now. But of course he has no place to go. This is his studio, his home, and she is a potential client: you don't walk out on that. She may be the one who walks through his door and gets it all started again. If she'd just walk through the door.

He turns to be sure everything is set—the coffee iced, the portfolio ready, the platter of cookies and fruit laid out—and surveys his space once more. It is essentially one large room, two stories tall, with the one big wall of window facing north. At the far end of the window, an overstuffed couch and a couple of chairs are gathered around an old steamer trunk. Beside them, a flight of stairs runs up to the door at the second-floor level, where a balcony along the back wall serves as an entrance hall. And under the balcony is his kitchen, compact as a galley on a ship, along with his bath and bedroom, all of it fit into the tight space with precision and economy.

The rest of the space is given over to his painting—an easel, surrounded by a glorious mess of jars and tubes and brushes, empty coffee cups, rags and palettes, crumpled bags once filled with pastry or sandwiches. Harry loves this corner of his world, the messiness of it. Even today, when it's straightened up, it still looks joyously untamed, rampant with color and life and juice, every crumpled tube of pigment oozing with possibilities. He is happy here, in his corner. If nowhere else, he is happy here.

But now his gaze falls on the easel, on the painting he's got underway—a red-headed man standing in a doorway, halfway in and halfway out—and he feels a violent tug in his stomach. He's had plenty of paintings fail before, but this is of a whole different order. Not because of the workmanship, but just because the painting falls so far short of what it needs to be, of what *Harry* needs it to be. It makes him question the very foundations on which he's built his life: why is he spending all his time trying to conjure people from the blankness of a canvas, trying to give the illusion of three dimensions when there are only two? He understands why *this* painting is finally raising all those questions—of course he understands—but that doesn't mean he's any closer to understanding the answers.

The doorbell rings at last, giving him a start. It always gives him a start, as abrupt and braying as it is. He strides to the intercom, presses the button. Yes?

It's Marjorie Davenport.

Ah, he says. Mrs. Davenport! Welcome. The lift is at the back of the lobby. Come up to the third floor.

He presses the other button and listens to hear the door swing open before he releases it. He checks himself in the mirror—hair artfully messed, clothes properly rumpled: he's done this enough to know that people don't want him to look too tidy—then he tugs his sleeves down to his wrists and climbs the stairs to his door. He considers whether to go to the lift and open the door when it arrives or to wait at his door, and be discovered. He leans against the jamb. He doesn't want to seem too eager; better his visitor comes to him. It is a mild form of a power play, like lowering your voice a bit to make your companion lean closer, listen.

The lift clanks to a stop and Marjorie Davenport opens the door, stepping into the hall. He likes her looks immediately. She is a handsome woman, probably in her middle forties. Hair cut short and business-like, but soft and loosely curled, a little blond highlight thrown in. Nicely tanned, big sunglasses, very good gold on her wrist. She is wearing a sleeveless summer dress and shouldering a little straw bag and somehow, in this deadly heat, she manages to look *crisp*. It occurs to him that she probably has an air-conditioned car. Then it occurs to him that in fact her whole life is probably climate-controlled.

She strides toward him, hand extended. Mr. Garrett.

Mrs. Davenport, welcome. Her handshake is firm. I see you didn't get trapped in the lift.

Does it happen?

A little too often, he laughs. He hopes she'll find that amusing but she doesn't seem to take notice.

I'm sorry I'm late, she says. I drove up from my sister's in Duxbury and I'm afraid I took a wrong turn. Boston is such a confusing town.

Yes, he says. It's because the streets were built to follow old cow paths. That's what happens when you leave your urban planning to livestock. Again, no amusement on her part. He gestures toward the door. Please come in.

As he steps aside to let her pass, he catches a whiff of her scent, something sweet and vaguely spicy, pleasant. He follows her onto the balcony and closes the door behind them.

Oh! she purrs. This is beautiful!

He hovers a little behind her, waiting to follow her down the stairs. It *is* a grand old building, he says. I'm very lucky to be here.

She plants her hands on the railing, apparently planning to stay here a moment. That window, she says, is fantastic!

Isn't it? he says. He moves next to her at the railing. We just got landmark status to keep them from building a high-rise there, cutting off our light.

She turns to him, shoulder up, shocked. They wanted to put a high-rise there? Right in front of you?

He nods wryly. Over the turnpike. We still have livestock doing our planning, only now it's asses instead of cows.

She tosses him an approving smirk and he feels he has finally scored a point. Feeling more confident now, he steps back and gestures to the stairs, then follows down behind her.

She arrives on the studio floor and turns about in circles, first one way then the other, admiring. Then she stops herself and looks at him. I'm sorry, she says. I get like this. I'm an interior designer.

Harry has a moment of dread. *A designer.* She's going to approach this painting the way she'd approach decorating a room—*I want these colors, this fabric, these drapes*—treating him like a hired hand, a functionary who only exists to execute her wishes. He doesn't want a list of specs to meet, he wants to be given the task of bringing someone to life on the canvas.

Would you care for iced coffee? he says. Iced tea?

Coffee would be wonderful.

Cream? Sugar?

I take it black.

Ah yes, he says. You're from the Midwest. He ducks into the kitchen, pulls out his kerchief and mops his brow.

Is that peculiar to the Midwest? she calls.

I think so, he calls back. Everyone here loads their coffee with cream and sugar. It's like they're trying to cover up the taste however they can. But I'm with you, he says, emerging from the kitchen with the tray of coffee, cookies and fruit. I like it straight and strong.

And are you from the Midwest? she says.

Originally from Michigan. He sits and holds up the flat of his palm—the Michiganders' handy map—and points to where his hometown is located, near the second knuckle; she allows as how she thinks she drove through it once on a summer vacation. They talk about what brought him to Boston (school), what took her to Cincinnati (her husband's job at Procter & Gamble), the way she learned about his work (the magazine ad, then his website).

He studies her features as they talk. The flat, almost Indian planes of her face, the almond shape of her eyes, the fullness of her lips, the bronze skin. He would love to paint her. And he finds that he rather likes her. She's a little on the formal side, but a lot of the people he deals with are formal. The rich, he has long since learned, *are* different from the rest of the world.

As they continue with their preliminaries, all their getting-to-know-each-other, it occurs to Harry that Marjorie Davenport seems to be a person who is used to negotiating; like a person, even, for whom every encounter is a negotiation. There is just the slightest delay with her, a sense that there are calculations going on behind her eyes. Which isn't surprising, under the circumstances: she is sizing him up, after all.

Just as he is sizing her up. And he thinks she is a good prospect. He's been painting portraits for fifteen years; he's gotten to the point he can tell who means business and who doesn't. He likes the way she responds to the paintings on his walls. She isn't just window-shopping, she seems to be looking for something. He even gets the feeling she might be ready to make a decision today.

So, he says at last. You are interested in a portrait?

She sets down her coffee. Yes.

She stares at the coffee a long moment. She seems to be gathering herself, as if she's about to address a difficult problem. I want a portrait of my children, she says at last, her eyes still on her glass. She takes a deep breath, folds her hands in her lap, then exhales and looks at him, smiling. My daughter, she says. And my son.

He nods. And how old are they?

My daughter is twenty-one, she says. She's a student here, just up the street at the Conservatory. She'll be a senior there this fall.

Ah. Well that will be convenient, he says. And the boy?

Michael.... She glances at the window, then down at her coffee. Michael just turned nineteen.

Well, he thinks. This is interesting. Two young people in the prime of life, flush with youthful exuberance. This might be a welcome change from all his dead professors and judges, all his little girls in Communion dresses.

And is Michael in Boston too?

No, she says. Michael... She shifts her weight. Well here's the problem, she says. Michael was...killed. Last fall.

Harry feels the air go out of him. I, he stammers. I'm sorry.

She looks down at her hands in her lap, twists her wedding ring.

How...?

It was an accident. She looks up. A hunting accident.

I'm sorry, he says, shifting gears, slowing down. He's used to navigating this moment with people—as a portrait artist, he ends up painting dead people a lot—but it always requires careful handling. It's like driving along a road and coming to a sudden, steep curve: all of a sudden he has to pay closer attention.

I do quite a bit of posthumous portraiture, he says at last. It can be a great help in remembering someone you've lost. It can help the healing process.

Yes, she says. Then more quietly, Yes.

When did Michael die?

Last Thanksgiving. He was home from his sophomore year at Dartmouth.

Harry shakes his head. This could be a difficult job, he thinks. It's one thing to paint a dead professor or dean or minister, someone in whom you can find the satisfaction of a life well lived. But this...

He remembers the painting he did of the four-year-old who had been killed in a plane crash. He had tried to capture him in a moment of perfect happiness—no past, no future, complete abandon, surrounding him with soap bubbles floating in the air. He'd taken the image from a photograph the boy's mother had given him, but then he'd played with it, seeing the boy's face, in part, through one of the soap bubbles, enormous in the foreground. Distorting the face, making it seem big and weightless, floating gently through space, sort of like the final image from the film *2001*, the fetus floating in space. Only not so corny, he thinks, and much better done.

Would you like to look at some portraits?

She sits up, eager. Yes.

He moves the tray to the floor and reaches for his portfolio, spreading it on the trunk before them, and turns on the overhead lamp. He proceeds through the book page by page and with each painting he tries to tell her a story—his repertoire is well rehearsed—something funny or touching about the experience of doing it, or about the client's reaction. Then, as she is drawn into it, he lets her turn the pages herself, setting her own pace.

He watches her carefully. Chances are good that she doesn't entirely know herself what she's looking for, and part of Harry's job here is to help her figure that out. And to help her toward an understanding of what she's looking for that will match what he can give her. It's always an interesting process, he thinks, this searching for common ground, for the match between expectations and abilities. She seems to linger the longest over the paintings Harry likes best himself, the paintings in which he feels he captured something essential about the subject. This is good. This is very good. He is feeling very encouraged here.

When she comes to the painting of the boy with the bubbles, she stops and stares at it. She seems to be quite taken with it. This is Joey, says Harry at last, slipping the comment in quietly. He was killed in a crash when he was four, coming home from his grandparents'. The parents were.... But he stops himself. He doesn't need to tell her how the parents felt.

He waits, and watches her watch the painting, almost as if she thinks it might move. The father told me, Harry murmurs, when I finished this painting...? He told me that I'd given him back the memory of his son. He'd had to identify the body.... Harry stops himself again, then goes on more quietly. He said the accident had taken away the memory of his son, but the painting had given it back. I think it was the most meaningful compliment I ever got.

She lingers on the image after he's finished his story, looking at it wistfully. He watches her, and waits. He notes the straining cords in her neck, the mask-like tension in her face.

This is the painting that came to my mind, he says softly. When you told me about Michael.

She nods as if she knew that. She reaches out to touch the boy's face. Harry stares at the finger touching the face, the face encased behind plastic, untouchable, untouched. He looks at the distortion of the boy's face in the painting, the glory in his eye, as if he is seeing something we can't see and is awed and mesmerized by it. Is it the bubble he sees? Or something else?

She closes the book and sits back. What do you think this will cost? she says. It is almost a chipper question.

Harry settles back beside her, tries to seem comfortable. Well, he says, it depends. On the size, for one thing. And it is a double portrait.... He glances out the window. Your daughter can make herself available?

Well, she sighs. That's one of the reasons I came to you. At least she can't argue it's inconvenient.

She has some resistance to this? says Harry, looking back at her.

Lindsay has resistance to everything, she says with a gently exasperated look. Everything having to do with me, at least. Lindsay doesn't quite *approve* of me. And she certainly doesn't approve of this painting.

Why?

She thinks it's ghoulish.

Well, Harry thinks. One of the subjects is dead and the other one doesn't want to be painted. This could be difficult indeed.

Do you have many photographs of Michael?

Tons. He was a beautiful boy, very photogenic. We were always taking pictures of him. He was a big star in school, in all kinds of sports and activities. A good student, enormously popular. A happy boy.... And here she falters. She looks down at her hands again.

Did you have a size in mind? A setting?

She sighs and looks up at him, grateful, it seems, for the distraction.

Big, I think. Maybe five feet square? Could that work for you?

He nods. The bigger the better.

I had thought of maybe having them at the piano. They used to sing together. Lindsay is quite an accomplished singer and has taken piano all her life. Michael was a good singer too, although he never took lessons. But he'd stand behind Lindsay and belt out the songs...I always loved that image of them together at the piano. It seemed to me to capture the essence of their relationship.

They had a good relationship?

She nods. It's one of the things I'm proudest of, what good friends they are. She stares at Harry a moment—aware, he thinks, that she just used the present tense—then glances out the window. I always wanted to capture that relationship in a picture, she says, her voice trailing off. Then she collects herself and looks back at Harry expectantly.

He slips a cookie into his mouth and dusts his hands on a napkin. He takes a sip of coffee, sits back. I should think a project like this would run about thirty thousand, he says. The large format, the special circumstances. He looks at her and holds her gaze.

She stares at him, poker-faced.

She can't be that surprised, he thinks; he has his rates on the website. But still, he holds his breath. Is he going to scare her off, here? He folds his hands in his lap, resisting the urge to equivocate. What the hell, he tells himself. They don't have to pay Michael's Dartmouth tuition anymore. It's a callousness that shocks even him, but it's a way of steeling himself. He hates this part of his business, naming his price.

How long do you think it would take? she says, hugging her pocketbook.

Ah-ha. She hasn't bolted for the door.

A portrait of that size...I should think about three months.

When do you think you could start?

This is good. She has not even mentioned the price. As soon as possible, he says. As soon as Lindsay's available.

She'll be coming back to school at the end of August.

We could start in early September, then.

So you could have it done by Christmas?

Yes, he says. I think so.

She stares at him a moment, thinking, then she looks out the window. What is going through her mind? he wonders. Is she considering other painters she's seen? Should he suggest meeting with Lindsay first? God no, what is he thinking? Give the girl a chance to queer the deal? Close it now. But how?

He watches her looking out the window and lets himself imagine what she's feeling in this moment, the immensity of her loss and the meagerness of this enterprise as a way of dealing with it. He feels it run right through him. Then he hears himself speaking.

When I was painting Joey, he says. The little boy with the bubbles? He clears his throat and it clears his head. I don't know what happened with that. But sometimes I had this sense of something here in the room with me.

She turns to look at him.

It was like a gentle presence, he says. Or just the suggestion of one. It was like something that was here just an instant ago and is suddenly gone, like a bubble that has just burst. He looks into her eyes and sees something he recognizes in there. He knew it was there. He looks away. It's hard to explain, he says. But I've been sort of hoping for an experience like that ever since.

Did he say that to her? Or just think it? He almost isn't sure. But when he looks up at her, she is staring at him oddly. She locks in with his gaze and searches his eyes. Then she seems to find her resolve. She reaches for her bag. It's fifty percent to begin? she says.

He breathes again, at last. Fifty percent up front, he says. Fifty percent on completion. I'll need everything you can give me in the way of photographs...

She takes out her checkbook. I'll write you a check for a thousand today and send a bank draft with the photos. Will that be all right with you?

That's fine, he says. That's fine. He is impressed with her decisiveness; she's used to doing business. No checking with the husband, no waffling back and forth. A decision, a check, a deal, chop-chop.

I'll have Lindsay get in touch with you as soon as she comes back to school.

I look forward to it.

She tears off the check and hands it to him, then puts the checkbook and her pen back into her bag and snaps it shut, hugging it to her hip. She stands and slings the strap over her shoulder. Well! she says, looking around. Well! This is very exciting!

I'm eager to get started, says Harry.

She flashes him a smile, a pact. She extends her hand. Me too.

You can send the photos any time, he says, as they make their way up the stairs.

I'll do it within the next two weeks.

There's no hurry, take your time. But I'll be watching for them.

When they reach the balcony she stops, surveying the whole gallery of portraits looking out from the walls. It must be strange, she muses. To have these people around you all the time.

Well, he murmurs. They are my people.

She nods, continues looking at them. Do you ever talk to them? she says. It is a wistful question, quiet.

Yes, he says softly. Sometimes.

She continues looking at them. And do they ever answer?

Harry waits a few beats. Sometimes.

She turns and looks at him. There is a recognition in her eyes, as if she can actually see inside him. It is such an urgent moment, so emphatically not calculated, that it catches

Harry off-guard. You take good care of my child, she whispers, and then she is out the door, leaving Harry standing there, stunned.

In a moment, he will follow her out to the lift and say his last goodbyes, then return to his studio to pick up after their meeting. But for now, here on the balcony, with her plea still ringing in the air, with his own heart suddenly seized, all Harry can do is wonder: which of her children did Marjorie Davenport mean?

2

When the plane begins to accelerate, the woman next to Marjorie grabs the arms of her seat. They've barely acknowledged each other so far. Marjorie nodded and gave her a pleasant look when she stood to let her in, then sat and went back to leafing through July's *Architectural Digest* as they taxied out on the tarmac.

But now, as the plane accelerates, she feels the woman tense. Marjorie turns and looks at her. There is no pretending she hasn't noticed, and she wouldn't want to pretend. The woman is clearly in crisis here, pressed to the back of her seat, eyes wide, sucking on her teeth. She senses Marjorie turning to her and rolls her head to the left, looking over at her wide-eyed, self-mocking.

I hate this part, she says.

Marjorie covers the woman's hand with her own. I know, she says. Me too. She isn't scared about flying, really, but she knows how this woman feels. So she presses herself to the back of her seat to copy the woman's posture in hopes that it will help to soothe her. It is something she can do, at least. If she can't deal with the bigger things, at least she can help this stranger through this little moment of fear.

The plane accelerates wildly, pressing them hard to the backs of their seats—it seems it's bound to fall apart any second just from the strain of it all—then the nose tips up and the bottom falls out and they are in the air, their stomachs sunk into their bowels, their hearts lifted into their throats.

The woman takes a deep breath and lets it out. Lord, I hate that part. She looks at Marjorie, embarrassed, relieved. Lifts her hand and squeezes it. Thank you.

The take-offs are the worst, says Marjorie. These things were never meant to fly.

It never used to bother me, says the woman, freeing her hand now to fuss with her clothes and hair.

Marjorie notices her nails are well done, and that they are her own nails, not appliqués, covered only with clear polish. They are beautiful hands, the color of coffee beans. The hair is hennaed and processed into a sort of pageboy. The lips are bright red. Lots of teeth and gums. Marjorie likes the presentation.

I used to love to fly, the woman goes on, her hands still flapping like birds. I used to love that feeling that my life was no longer in my control. *Whatever you want, Lord, I'm in your hands. There's nothing I can do about it. I'll just sit back here and relax.* She looks at Marjorie, eyes wide. I used to think flying was *relaxing.* Then one of her hands plops down on Marjorie's arm. But you know, she says confidentially, the older I get the more I have to lose. I think that is the difference. I don't *like* that loss of control anymore.

Marjorie smiles and nods. *The older I get, the more I have to lose.* It is an interesting thought. She's aware that a year ago she would have agreed without even thinking about it, but now it is a question: Hasn't she lost everything already? Rationality rushes in to assure her she's got a lot left to lose—Lindsay, David, life itself—but her heart is not convinced. And God, she hates being ambushed by this question several times a day. Every time she gets free of it, every time she forgets for a moment what has happened to her, something comes along and reminds her.

Oh! the woman goes on. Why did I *ever* leave Cincinnati?

Do you live in Cincinnati? says Marjorie, glad to have a change of subject.

I grew up there, the woman says. I'm going to visit my sister. I haven't seen her for a couple of years. I don't like to fly. She explodes in laughter, exposing her teeth and gums. Or maybe you knew that already.

Marjorie tells her she is just returning from seeing her sister in Boston, and it seems to give the woman license to launch into her life story. She tells Marjorie all about her sister, about her sister's children, about her own children, about her life. Marjorie listens politely, mildly interested. This is what she had hoped would *not* happen, that she would get trapped in conversation for the next few hours. But her magazine isn't interesting, and having just been attacked by her own feelings again she's grateful for the momentary distraction.

Now the woman is taking her billfold out of her pocketbook, showing Marjorie pictures of her children, pudgy little tootsie-roll fingers, gaping toothless grins. Now her nieces and nephews, older and skinnier. The boy in a white graduation gown, the girl with her hair tied in strange directions. And Marjorie finds herself opening her shoulder bag, as well. Taking out her billfold, showing off her pictures.

This is my daughter, says Marjorie. She's going to school in Boston now. She wants to be an actress.

Oh isn't she *pretty,* the woman says, taking the billfold in her hands to have a closer look. She *could* be a movie star, I can see it!

Marjorie brags about Lindsay's voice, her piano playing, her dancing. The woman makes all the appropriate sounds, all the coos of approval, then catches a glimpse of the photo beneath and flips the sleeve to look at it.

And is this your son? she says.

Marjorie hesitates a moment. Yes, she says, faltering. Yes. That's Michael.

Isn't he handsome! says the woman. My, my. He *is* a handsome boy.

Yes, says Marjorie timidly. Yes, he's very handsome.

Is he in college too?

Marjorie stares at the photo of Michael, smiling brightly at the camera, the essence of youth and promise. He's a sophomore at Dartmouth, she says.

I bet he's a lady killer, that one.

Every cell in Marjorie's body tightens. She reaches to take the wallet back, then gazes down at the picture, smoothing her hand across the sleeve as if she were brushing the hair from his eyes. He was on the wrestling team in high school, she hears herself say. They went to state championships.

And what's he studying now?

Marjorie stares at the photo. He hasn't declared his major yet but he'll probably go into business. He's pledged a fraternity, he's dating a girl from California. She continues on, she can't stop herself. He rooms with a boy from Saskatchewan. He'll do his junior year abroad.

The woman listens, nodding, smiling.

Marjorie stares at the picture. He'll be home for Christmas, she murmurs.

The flight attendant arrives with his cart and Marjorie asks for a scotch. She fishes the money out of her wallet while he sets out the bottle, the plastic glass with the ice, the little bag of pretzels. She hands him the bills and he thanks her for the right change, then moves along.

The conversation has been broken; this is her chance to close it down. She puts her wallet back in her bag and takes out the paperback book she started on the beach at her sister's. She sets the book beside her drink and pours the scotch over the ice. It's only 3PM, but on a plane you're in limbo anyway. And if David can drink scotch every night, and sometimes in the daytime too, she can certainly have one on the plane. The first sharp taste of it brings her around, almost like smelling salts. All at once her world is small again, contained on this seat-back table. Bottle, pretzels, plastic cup. Familiar things. Manageable things.

She feels the woman next to her stir, senses she is about to speak, so she picks up the book and opens it, trying to pick up the thread again. It is a story about a German woman and a fifteen-year-old boy, having an affair. It all seems very authentic, what she can get of it. How a fifteen-year-old boy would feel making love with a full-grown woman. But she doesn't get more than a couple of pages before she has to stop and wonder: Did Michael ever make love? Did he taste that pleasure before he died? And was it a pleasure? Or was it a sordid ordeal, something to be ashamed of? What was his experience of life? How little she knew of him, really, she thinks. She closes her eyes and lays her head back.

She tries to let her mind drift and finds herself thinking about Harry Garrett, that painter. There was something so *moist* about him, she thinks, as if his skin were so tight it was squeezing the juice right out of him. And he had such a gingerly quality to him, something careful and old fashioned, at odds with his loosely muscled frame, his messed-up hair, his paint-stained nails. He seemed uncomfortable in his body; there was a hesitancy, a tentativeness in his movement that suggested he didn't quite trust what he might do next. But she liked the intelligence in his eyes, and the soulfulness. And she certainly liked his paintings. The lighting, the atmosphere, the sense that the subjects might move any second.

Still, she is amazed she agreed to pay him so much, so quickly. It feels a little dangerous, somehow, especially considering Lindsay's resistance. But what do you do when your son dies? How do you respond to that? Do you just sit there and take it? At least she has made an effort to do something to move them along. Maybe it's stupid, maybe it's silly. But at least she has done something.

And besides, there was something about that man. When he talked about that painting of the boy who had been killed in a plane crash. When he talked about the process of painting it, of feeling a presence. There was something in his voice when he said that. She felt something in her heart. It felt like a sailboat coming about, heading up into the wind. A rock and sway, a heft of great weight, and *boom*. The decision was made. She felt a hole open up in her heart, felt a wind rush through it. And he held her gaze steady. He held her steady as surely as if he'd reached out and clasped his forearm to hers.

She settles lower into her seat and takes a long, deep breath. She feels for a moment as if she has stumbled into a clearing in the woods, a place with a view and a place to sit, and remembers coming across just such a place on a hike with David last fall, after they'd taken Michael to school. A little clearing on a hilltop with a view of a village below, a perfect little New England village nestled into the valley, its bright white steeple pointing at the sky, surrounded with hills upholstered in orange and yellow and red like a nubbly tweed. There was a bench, and a brook nearby, gurgling its happy sounds. So she and David sat and looked out, content and slightly exhausted, like two old farmers who have just finished bringing in the wheat. They didn't speak, they just sat and looked. Leaning against each other slightly, actually holding hands.

Well, Old Girl, David said at last. I guess it's just you and me now.

As Marjorie rides up the escalator she can see David waiting for her, tossing his car keys over his fingers as if they were worry beads. He is tall and trim for his age, wearing plaid shorts and a polo shirt, loafers with no socks—just the way he has always dressed. She likes to see him dressed this way, likes to see he still looks good in the kinds of clothes he used to wear when she fell in love with him. She likes the memories it brings back of afternoons at football games, evenings at fraternity parties, study dates and drinking in pubs, everything very loud. And she likes the stretch of memories filling the years between then and now. The babies, the cars, the apartments, the houses. Twenty-two years together. It all jumbles into one big memory, like a mural in which all of the events are occurring at once. And in all the memories, he's wearing these clothes—plaid shorts and a polo shirt—even when everyone around him was wearing bell bottoms and tinted glasses.

Timeless, he called it. Classic.

Unadventurous, she teased him.

When she gets to the top he gives her a hug, casual and possessive. But when she kisses him, it feels to her as if they're a couple of marionettes clanking together in an awkward embrace.

Have a good trip? he says.

I did. It was very successful.

How was the birthday party?

Lots of fun, she bubbles. They had a campfire on the beach and everyone sang old camp songs. Everyone asked after you. She pushes her sunglasses up on her head. What did you do this weekend?

Oh, David sighs, not much. Bernie and Jo asked me over last night, but I didn't really feel like it. I just read the paper this morning. Went to an open house this afternoon.

Oh? she says, perking up. Whose?

No, not a party, he says. A real estate open house.

She looks at him, surprised. Why?

I was just poking around.

She studies his profile, perplexed. Where was it?

Lytle Place.

Lytle Place? Downtown?

It had a beautiful view.

But Lytle *Place*.

I was just looking.

When they are finally out on the highway, successfully merged and cruising along, Marjorie finally tells him her news. Well! she says brightly, turning to him. I commissioned us a portrait!

He glances at her. You did it?

Yep. I went up to the painter's studio yesterday, in Boston. You should *see* his studio, David. It's absolutely beautiful! And he's just around the corner from Lindsay's school. I still can't believe I found such a wonderful painter so close by. It's like this painting is just meant to be.

What's the guy's name?

Harry Garrett. You remember I showed you his stuff on the web? He's quite well thought of. But it doesn't really matter. I think his work is wonderful. And I got a very good feeling from him.

How much is it going to cost?

Umm.... she says. She clears her throat, gives him a thousand-watt show-biz smile, and drops the bomb.

David looks at her and his eyes go wide, then his gaze drifts back to the road as if he's been stunned by a blow to the head.

She touches his shoulder, to steady him. I'll pay it from my account, she says. You don't need to worry about it.

No, he says, still dazed. It's OK.

You mean it? she says. You think it's OK?

Yeah, he says. It's fine. If it'll make you happy, it's worth it.

She settles back into her seat. I decided to have them at the piano, the way they always used to sing there together? Don't you think that will be nice?

Sure, he says. I guess.

Well *tell* me, she says. What do you think? I mean, if you don't like that we can do something else. We could put them outdoors. We could make it more formal....

No, he says. The piano is fine. If you want them at the piano, that's where they should be.

But I want you to feel a part of this. I want this to be your painting too. She leans across the seat toward him. I think it's going to be good for us. She searches his profile. Don't you think?

David nods, non-committal.

I know it's a lot of money, but that's what these things cost. And like I said, I got a good feeling from him....

Don't worry about it, says David calmly. It's OK. It's fine.

He stares down the highway, hypnotized. His voice sounds to Marjorie like the voice on one of Lindsay's old dolls—you pull the string and get a recording. She squares herself in her seat again, gazing down the highway at whatever it is David's staring at.

At least it's something, she says, more or less to herself.

• • •

When they get home, David disappears into the family room to watch a baseball game while Marjorie sifts through her mail, laid out for her on the dining room table. There's nothing interesting there—catalogues, bills, circulars, a couple of checks from clients and a long-overdue fabric sample.

She carts her suitcase upstairs and takes a long hot shower to wash off the closeness from the trip, then pulls on shorts and a T-shirt and pads down to the kitchen barefoot to get herself a Diet Coke.

What's the score? she says, wandering into the family room and laying a hand on the back of David's neck.

Hmm? he says. I don't know. It's not a very good game.

She notices he has a tumbler full of scotch at his side. You want to go for a walk? she says. It's a beautiful day outside.

You know, he says, I'm kind of bushed. He reaches up and takes her hand. Can I get a raincheck?

Sure. Of course. I was just feeling at loose ends.

She glances at the game on TV, then wanders back to the kitchen and out to the foyer. She stands there looking into the living room, pristine in its uselessness. There was a time when there were parties here. Dinner parties, cocktail parties, pre-game parties, post-game parties, New Years' Day open houses with lots of laughing and lively chatter, David telling jokes in the corner, calling out to people across the room. They managed a room like a team of border collies, she and David, instinctively working together to shape the contours of a party. No wallflowers at their parties, everyone had a good time or else. But now there is just the tick of the clock on the mantle. That and the faint roar of the TV crowd in the family room, the chatter of the announcers above it.

She turns to go back to the family room, gets halfway across the foyer, then turns and goes back to the living room.

She marches to the couch and steps up on it to remove the Japanese screen from the wall above it, then steps back and looks at the empty wall, trying to imagine a five-by-five painting hanging there. It will totally change the room, she knows, and that will set off other changes to accommodate it. Changes in colors and textures, the position of the furniture. She begins to try to imagine it, how everything will change, but until she sees the painting, of course, she can't even begin.

Energized, she heads up the stairs to the sitting area at the top and surveys the wall of photos there. There must be over fifty of them, all framed and fitted together. She removes the photo of Michael and his dad playing golf at Pebble Beach. She removes the high school graduation photo. She removes the shot of Michael poised in his wrestling uniform. She sets the pictures in the chair, then sits on the floor and pulls a photo album out of the bookcase.

She opens it on the floor before her and starts flipping through the pages, searching for good pictures of him, but she doesn't get very far with it before she starts to slow. It's as if there's a force of gravity in these books different from the world around them. As if she has passed into another dimension, a denser atmosphere requiring much more effort to move. The pages grow heavier and harder to turn and she feels herself begin to implode, to crumble from within like a building that's been dynamited. The implosion continues, and continues, until she feels she is falling into herself, collapsing into a black hole, tunneling down to one bright hot dot, one tiny pin-prick of herself, a substance so dense it doesn't exist.

3

Harry perches on his couch with the photographs spread out before him, a mug of coffee in his hand. He has looked at these photos before, when they first arrived so carefully wrapped, then wrapped again in their insured package, a bank draft enclosed with a note from Marjorie Davenport saying how excited she was to be embarking on this project with him, how she knew that Michael would be pleased too. It was a simple little note, pretty much standard issue, but he appreciated her form, and her monogrammed stationery. He also appreciated the check.

He spreads the loose photos before him now to refresh his memory. His first impression had been that the boy was certainly beautiful. When his mother had called him that, Harry had taken it with a grain of salt. Doesn't every mother think her son is beautiful? But in this case, it was objectively so—he had inherited her cheekbones, her eyes, the fullness of her lips. And from his father, perhaps, he had olive skin, a gleaming white smile, hair so black it was almost blue.

But Harry's immediate impression was that this boy was not knowable, in some way. Because his beauty was so distracting? Or was it the sense of withholding in the eyes, the sense that there was someone behind that face, looking out from some lair? The way eyes look when seen through a mask, when they're set in a different plane and made of a different substance than the surrounding features. There was a whole world behind that face, Harry thought, and you couldn't say that of every face. When you looked at some people, you felt what you saw was pretty much what you got. But this face had mystery in it, secrets. He loved the prospect of painting it. He wished he could do it in the flesh.

When the buzzer rings he jumps, holding the photo quickly away from him for fear he'll spill coffee on it. He ferries the coffee to the kitchen and sets it in the sink, then answers the intercom.

Who is it?

Lindsay Davenport.

Ah! he says, excited. Come in!

He presses the button to buzz her in and listens for the door to swing open, then climbs the stairs to wait for her, positioning himself by the door, waiting to be discovered. He is nervous about this meeting. It's like having a blind date, but worse: more like an arranged marriage. Who are these two people between whom others have made promises? Are they going to like each other at all? Is he going to want to paint this girl? He thinks of the check discreetly folded into the seashell stationery: yes, he'll want to paint this girl.

The lift arrives, but the door doesn't open. Is she stuck? Does she need help? He starts to move forward, but then the door bursts open and she blunders out, an enormous bag on her shoulder. It's too late for him to regain his composure; she's caught him off-base, away from home-free, halfway between here and there. She turns and looks at him.

Harry?

Yes, he says, laughing nervously. Yeah. Harry Garrett. Hi. He holds out his hand.

She cocks her weight on one hip, slides her thumb up the strap of her bag to reposition it on her shoulder. Yeah, she says. I'm Lindsay. She doesn't shake his hand.

She is small, one might say petite, but she seems to take up a lot of space. Her hair is pulled into two ragged ponytails sprouting out of her head like weeds, held with plain brown rubber bands. She is wearing gym shoes and black tights and a sweatshirt with the arms cut off and the neckhole enlarged, and Harry can see that she has a good body, athletic and well-toned, still tan from her summer break. He can also see that she is absolutely unimpressed with him.

You gonna invite me in? she says.

Oh, he says. Yeah, of course. This way.

He steps back to let her pass, gesturing to the open door— she smells of sweat and tobacco, he notes—then follows her onto the balcony. She pauses a moment, glances around—*Huh,* she grunts—then heads down the stairs, her bag banging off the wall in such a way that Harry's afraid she might dislodge one of his paintings.

When she reaches the studio floor she drops her bag beside the couch and stares at the photos of Michael spread out on the trunk. Harry pauses on the stairs to watch, still as a setter on point. She stares at the photos for a long moment, then looks up at him. You got any coffee? she says irritably.

He hurries down the stairs as if he's been caught doing something he shouldn't be doing, and disappears into the kitchen. Why is he hurrying? he wonders. Why is he feeling so nervous?

Cream? he calls to her. Sugar?

Both.

I see you've outgrown your Midwestern roots, he says as he brings out a tray with the cups, the cream, the sugar, the cookies.

Huh?

Your Midwestern roots. Midwesterners drink their coffee black. Or at least your mother does, and I do.

Midwesterners do a lot of things, she says. She doesn't seem happy about it.

He watches her as she turns the coffee into some sort of witches' brew, so full of foreign substances as to be unrecognizable. Well, he says. You've acclimated.

Huh?

To New England. The cream and sugar.

She looks at him as if she hasn't a clue what he's talking about. He drops it and returns to the kitchen to get a bowl of grapes he's set out. When he returns she is slouched in one of the chairs, lighting a cigarette.

I'd prefer it, he says, if you didn't smoke here.

She shakes out the match and looks at him, still holding it in the air, blue smoke curling up. She holds her breath, then exhales in a gush, creating a thundercloud of fumes.

Well, she says. Then we're even. I'd prefer not to be here at all.

She mashes her cigarette out on her saucer, lays the smoldering match on the trunk. Harry watches this with amazement, annoyance and then with some amusement. He goes back to the kitchen, gets a new saucer, brings it back to the steamer trunk, exchanges it for the mess she's created, picks up the match and takes it all back to the kitchen, to dump in the garbage.

I do accept tips, he says politely, as he cleans up after her.

She pops a grape into her mouth, seems to be searching for a retort and seems irritated that she can't find one.

So, Harry says, returning to the couch and taking a seat. We meet at last.

She arranges herself in her chair. What are you gonna want from me?

Well, he says, settling back. For starters, why don't we get acquainted?

I've got class in half an hour.

Oh, he says, taken aback. Well. I had hoped we might have longer.

Sorry, she says, taking great care to be sure he knows she isn't. Has she always been such a bitch? he wonders.

You're not very pleased about this project.

Hey, she says. Wanna be a millionaire?

Sorry?

She sits up and leans forward to take another sip of coffee. You've got all the answers right so far.

Why is that?

I guess you're just smart.

I mean why does this project bother you so much?

She freezes with a cookie halfway to her mouth. Because my brother is dead, she says. And my mother wants to turn him into interior décor.

Well, says Harry, shifting his weight. I'd like to think this painting will be something more than simply décor.

Yes, she says. I'm sure you would.

He holds her gaze a long moment, letting the tension dissipate.

I'm sorry about your brother, he says.

She stares at him, then looks away. She sets the cookie down, pushes herself to her feet and crosses to the window.

I'm told you paint dead people a lot, she says, turning to look up at the paintings on the studio walls. All those people dead?

Not all, he says. Some of them.

She wanders over to the easel to look at the painting he's working on. Harry feels uncomfortable seeing her in his private corner, he hasn't invited her to look. Doesn't she understand that this is invasive? But of course she understands: that's exactly why she's doing it. He takes a deep breath and watches her with a kind of clinical interest.

This one dead? she says.

Harry swallows. Yes.

Who is it? she says.

A friend.

Her gaze flicks up at him as if she has suddenly understood something, then she smirks and wanders toward the kitchen. You live here, Harry?

I do.

Small, she says, peering back into the living quarters.

At this point he has given up trying to control this conversation, or even to try to steer it. He is clearly watching a performance, so he just sits back and takes it in. Will she actually go into his bedroom? Will she look behind his shower curtain? Explore his medicine cabinet? She might very well do any of that. He watches her, interested and detached, feeling a bit disdainful of this preposterous pose but willing to wait it out. What else can he do, after all?

She comes back to the edge of the kitchen, leans against the wall, looking at him.

You live here alone?

I do.

She considers him a moment, seems to be taking his measurements. You gay, Harry?

He lets his gaze settle in on her, slightly cocks an eyebrow. Actually, I'm a monk, he says.

What's that mean?

It means that I don't sleep with anybody.

Nobody at all?

He shakes his head.

Huh, she grunts. How selfish.

She comes back to her chair, and sits. She points to the photos with her chin. So what do you think of my brother?

He looks like he was a fine young man.

She nods, slightly dazed. He was.

Do you always wear your hair like that?

She glances upward, fingers her weeds. No, she says. I've got class. I've gotta go pretty soon.

What class have you got?

Modern dance.

You like it?

She bristles. I like it well enough. She reaches for her cigarettes, then puts them back on the table. What is it you're going to need from me, Harry?

I'll want to take some pictures of you, he says. And do some life sketches. We'll need to find a piano similar to the one you've got at home, at least in size, so I can get some shots of you in relation to it. Can we do that at your school?

She shrugs.

Or I can ask around.

There's lots of pianos at school, she says. I can probably find you one.

Another thing I'd like to do?

She waits.

I'd like to talk about your brother.

She taps her cigarettes on the table. I can probably find a piano, she says.

When Lindsay finally gets home and gets through all the locks on her door, she finds Bobby washing dishes and singing along to *A Chorus Line*. Bobby is always singing and dancing; he seems born to be a song-and-dance man. If there were room any more in this world, he laments, for a song-and-dance man.

Sometimes he says he thinks he'll end up offering perfume samples to middle-aged matrons at a department store. But he sings and dances his way through it all—eyes huge, his enormous mouth stretched wide, his copper skin glistening.

Anita! he cries when he sees her. *Felicitaciones!*

Huh?

They just posted it! he cries, rushing toward her to give her a kiss. Honey, you got the part!

I got Anita? she gasps.

He grabs her shoulders with his wet hands and his head hammers up and down in excited nods.

Lindsay collapses on the couch, letting out a startled little laugh.

Well aren't you *excited?* Bobby cries. This is the part you wanted!

She looks up at him helpless, exhausted. I can't believe it, she says. I beat out Linda Lopez?

Oh Honey, you *gotta* believe it! You are gonna be a *star!*

Lindsay glances around the apartment, breathless, then looks at Bobby. What did you get?

He strikes a macho pose. I'm a *Shark!* Gonna beat me some white boy *ass!*

He pounces down on the couch beside her and they gossip a while about the show, who got what part, when rehearsals start, but within a few minutes Lindsay feels overcome with exhaustion. She pushes herself to her feet and staggers toward her room.

Don't you wanna smoke? says Bobby.

Nah, she says. I'm just gonna crash.

Sweet dreams, Cupcake.

She smiles, almost in spite of herself, then closes the door behind her and plops down on the bed amid all her dirty clothes. She doesn't know why she's so exhausted. She ought to be exhilarated from landing such a juicy part, but all she wants to do is collapse. She closes her eyes and tries to sleep but the music is thrumming through the wall, so she turns on her back and stares up at the ceiling. Then abruptly she fishes her phone from her bag and speed dials her dad at work.

Hey sweetheart! he says when he comes on the line.

Hey Dad! she chirps, trying to sound energetic.

What's up?

Well, she says. I've got some good news.

I could use some of that.

I got a great part in the fall show.

Lindsay! he cries. That is great!

She tells him about the play and the part, all the singing and dancing required, her big scene at the end. It takes a lot more energy than she feels she really has right now but for her father, she always rallies. That's just the way it has always been. She has basked in her father's adoration all her life—it's probably part of what has turned her into a performer, having such a rapt audience.

Aw Lindsay, he says, right on cue. That is wonderful. That is really wonderful.

There's a fawning quality in his voice that makes her a little uncomfortable, reminding her of the way he seems to have become an old man of late—not physically, but emotionally. He seems thinner in his psyche, his aura. Watered down, and tired. She struggles to prop him up but she feels like she's auditioning and she's not going to get the part.

I am so proud of you, he purrs.

She sits up and runs her hand through her hair, scrambling for a different topic. I went to see that painter today.

Oh yeah? he says. The portrait guy? How did that go?

She slumps against the wall. I think it's a stupid idea.

Lindsay, he says. We talked about this. If it'll help your mother, then do it.

But what does she think this is going to accomplish? Does she think this will bring him alive again?

There is an awkward pause. She simply wants a picture of the two of you, her father says softly.

Well it's weird, she mutters.

What's the guy like?

He's weird too. She searches the bedclothes for her cigarettes. I don't know how to explain it. He's got this cute little face—he's *cute*—but he lives alone in this little studio surrounded with all these pictures. It's like being in a mausoleum.

Did he start the painting?

No, we just talked. She lights a cigarette and exhales it toward the window in a thick blue stream, recalling how anal the guy was about smoking in his studio. He wants to do some sketches and take some pictures, she says. She wants us at the piano.

I know.

I think it's creepy.

It won't kill you, says her father, and then a silence falls between them, sucking the air out of both of them, and they are both, for a moment, lost.

Well, he mumbles. I should get back to work.

How's Mom? she blurts out, to hold him there.

Oh, he says. She's OK, I guess. She's keeping busy. She's getting a lot of work right now.

Oh, says Lindsay. That's good, I guess.

Gotta pay for that painting somehow!

Lindsay feels a sting of shame. Her parents are putting out a lot of money for this thing, the least she could do is cooperate. She looks around her room, at the clothes strewn on the furniture, on the floor, the dirty laundry in the corner. I ought to clean my room, she muses.

You living like a college student?

Well I'm living, she says. And I'm a student.

And then there is that silence again. And soon enough, they hang up.

Lindsay pulls a jacket off the floor and lays it over her shoulders, then pounds on the wall with her fist. When Bobby lowers the music, she snuggles into the bedclothes, frowning, her hands curled up by her mouth like a squirrel nibbling on a nut, feeling even more exhausted than she was before the call.

It comes over her often, without warning, this overwhelming fatigue. She felt it repeatedly during the summer, living with her parents again as if she were still a child. It was like a morgue in that house this summer, the pall over the place. Her mother hovering over her like a Red Cross helicopter, trying to anticipate her every conceivable need, and when she didn't have any needs, making them up herself. It was the most oppressive place she has ever been in her life, with Michael's room there at the end of the hall, frozen in time like a shrine. Every time she walked down the hall she had to look at that door. Every time, she half expected Michael to open it up and ask her to come in and listen to the latest Pearl Jam or Nirvana. Every time she walked down that hall, she felt her heart rise up in anticipation of it and every time the door just stood there as if it were nailed shut.

Once she walked down the hall and actually stood in front of the door. It was about four o'clock in the afternoon, she was home alone. The house seemed unnaturally quiet; there was the buzz of a lawnmower in the distance. But in the house, the air hung heavy, like drapes. She stood at the door a moment, then reached out and pushed it ajar. She looked at the sunlight on the floor inside, the way it bent when it hit the rug then bent again to bathe the bed. It seemed warm, inviting, as if Michael were in there in some form, welcoming her memories, willing to share them with her. She thought she might have a moment with him, surrounded with his things, maybe even his smell. She thought she might touch things, linger there, begin to find some peace with him, maybe listen to see if he'd whisper to her. Crossing the threshold into his room might be like crossing a larger threshold, like crossing into a middle space, a meeting ground between here and there where anything might happen. She didn't know if she dared it; it seemed somehow dangerous. But she pushed the door open further, watching the room swing into view—the pennants, the trophies, the books, the posters, the little bookcase he'd made in woodshop, the bulletin board of clippings and photos. His varsity letters. The clothes in the closet. The empty aquarium.

The aquarium had been his favorite thing; she remembered the Christmas he'd gotten it, the hours he'd spent assembling it, setting up his little diorama—the diver, the treasure chest, the shipwreck, the plastic chair and TV from her dollhouse, the decapitated doll. He made up stories about the fish. Hector and Phineas and Lucille, she remembered. Dogwood and Dagwood and Lydia. They were full of lusts and jealousies, romance and intrigue. She remembered when Phineas turned belly up, Michael had spent an entire week sleuthing out who had done it. He finally announced, at dinner one night, it was the headless doll: she'd run out of Mrs. Paul's fish sticks.

By the time he entered high school, he had stopped making up the stories—he was too distracted with other things—but he kept the aquarium going, sometimes just sitting there in the dark, staring at its garish colors and hypnotizing bubbles.

The sight of the tank now empty, its sides all milky with scum, no trace at all of the color, the movement, the stories, the vividness that had been there...it was just an empty glass box, a featureless thing at a garage sale. It made her heart go hollow, as fragile and empty as the box itself, and she backed out into the hall again and pulled the door shut, wiping her hands on her jeans.

Lindsay flips onto her back again. There is too much jazz in her nerve endings, her breath is coming too short to rest. She can't just lie here like this anymore. If she can't sleep she has to get up. Through the wall she can hear the faint strumming of *One Singular Sensation*. She catapults to her feet, throws a scarf around her neck, flings open her door and sashays out into the living room, gliding about in time to the music, like the Singular Sensation she's always tried so hard to be. Bobby waltzes out from the kitchen, doing a kick step to back her up, fluttering his hands in the air, his smile as wide as a keyboard.

4

Whn the girl shows up for their meeting one week later, Harry likes what he sees. She's prepared herself for him this time. Her dark hair is loosely curled and combed, softly framing her face. She is wearing a little make-up, just enough to bring her face into focus. And she is dressed in an actual dress, a simple little number, all black, that shows off her collarbone and her curves and the attractive square of her shoulders. It flutters gracefully when she walks. She is even wearing high heels.

Harry, she says as she walks toward him.

Lindsay, he says, bowing slightly.

She brushes past him through the door—she smells of something familiar; is it a men's cologne?—then he follows her onto the balcony, closing the door behind them.

You look very nice, he says.

She turns to him and smiles, obviously pleased, then proceeds down the stairs. Harry is surprised and encouraged by the change in her attitude. He follows her down—she does have terrific legs, he notes—and gets her seated on the couch, then brings out the coffee and cookies and fruit and sits in the chair across from her.

So how have you been? he asks.

She shrugs. I guess I'm doing OK.

He waits for her to go on. She doesn't.

Maybe she isn't feeling quite as cooperative as he'd hoped.

Is this how you usually wear your hair? he says, leaning forward to pour them coffee.

When it's clean.

He hands her a cup and studies her for a moment. It is a good style for you, he says. It sets off your jaw and your neck. You have a good strong jaw line.

She seems to preen a bit under his gaze, elongating her neck, and it makes him a little self-conscious. Do you mind if I sketch as we talk? he says. Without waiting for a response he picks up his pad from the floor beside him, flips it open and sets it on his knees, then pulls a pencil from his pocket.

Do you want me to take off my clothes?

He looks up at her, surprised, uncertain if she's joking or not. She looks back at him with sparkling eyes. Is that mirth in her eyes, or something else? He can't tell what she's after, so he gives her no reaction at all.

That won't be necessary, he says, utterly poker-faced.

He turns his attention back to his paper and begins to draw. The pad, tilted on his knees, like a drawbridge slightly raised.

Could you just look over here? he says, holding his pencil beside his ear. A little more to the left.

She complies, and he begins sketching again. He concentrates on her jaw line, the shape of her head and the way it sits on her neck. He works quickly, in broad gestures.

Tell me about your classes, he says, and she starts to talk, at last. She is studying acting, dance and literature. She is a senior this year, almost. She has a part in an upcoming show. She wants to be an actress, probably in the musical theater, but these days you have to be prepared to do anything.

Even porn? Harry wonders, still thinking about that off-the-wall remark about taking off her clothes. He chalks it up to the fact she's an actress, a natural-born exhibitionist. And the fact of that does seem to work in his favor. She doesn't seem to mind being stared at.

He flips the page, to start a new sketch. Could you lean back against that pillow? he says. Put your head back, stretch your neck a bit?

She does exactly as he says. She takes direction well. Her neck is long and graceful and white against the fabric of the pillow. She seems to offer it up, as if to a vampire.

Is this the way you're going to paint me? she laughs. Stretched out on the couch?

This is just a series of quick sketches to get us limbered up, he says.

Oh. Like stretching before you dance.

I guess. I just want to explore how your body moves, the way you fit together. This is also just a way for us to get comfortable together. Maybe I could sketch you dancing sometime?

You might.

He concentrates on her neck, the long graceful line, the way it joins the shoulder. The slope of her arm, the hand in her lap. He loves this stage, the quick sketching. Nothing he does really matters; it's all just hypothetical, all just exploration. In some ways he never feels quite so free as when he's doing quick sketches. There's a wonderful recklessness to it that he doesn't ordinarily experience. A messiness, an abandon. He leans into the curves of his pencil as he imagines a racecar driver leans into the curves of the road, and soon his entire body is engaged in exploring hers.

So how come you always sleep alone? she says, apropos of nothing.

Harry looks up, confused. Uh, he says. Well? He clears his throat. It's not like the world is exactly knocking down my door. He stares at her, wondering what she's thinking.

Sounds lonely, she says at last.

He clears his throat again. I get by.

She lifts her hand and gazes at her bracelet, turning her wrist this way and that. Is that enough? she says absently. Getting by?

Harry shifts his weight, then turns the page of his sketchbook. Could you turn and lean on the arm of the couch? he says. Yeah. Exactly like that. He begins to sketch again, slowly. So, he says. Why don't you tell me about this show you're in?

She starts talking about the play. It seems to involve a lot of singing and dancing, lots of drama. My boyfriend gets killed in the end, she says.

It sounds like a *tour de force,* he says, but he is only half-listening, the way he sometimes listens to the radio when he's painting.

I'm bored, she says suddenly.

He looks up, breaking his concentration.

Can we have a little music?

Sure, he says. Of course.

She gets up and turns on his radio, then tunes it to KISS 108. The music is foreign, disjointed—it doesn't seem to fit in this studio—but it gives him another clue to who she is. She starts to wander around the room, moving a little in time to the music. He likes the challenge of this, trying to capture the sense of movement with a single line, a gesture. This is the kind of exercise he always loved, in school. But now that he's working professionally, it doesn't happen much anymore. Judges and deans and dead people don't do a lot of moving around.

As she moves, her body becomes more liquid, her bearing more electric. She seems to love having his attention and resent it at the same time, as if it isn't quite the kind of attention she's looking for but she'll settle for it anyway, in lieu of something else. And as she moves, he sees the kind of attention she wants is more personal, maybe more sexual. He imagines she might like it if he started dancing with her, if he got up from his chair and started to follow her around the room like an animal in heat. He hasn't had a woman present herself like this in a very long time and it makes him a little uncomfortable. How is he supposed to react to this? She's half his age, and a client. Worse: the *daughter* of a client. Of course, the beauty of this work is that you don't ever really have to react, you're just there to observe and interpret. But still, this is unsettling. He lets the movement go on a bit longer, then sets his pad aside.

OK, he says, turning off the radio. I'm going to need you to sit still again while I take some pictures.

He sits her on a stool by the window, positioning her just so. He is in control of her again, the camera safely between them. He starts shooting, moving around her, creeping in close then backing away. *Click, click, click, click.* He loves the sound his camera makes, the crisp efficiency of it. He concentrates on that sound, and it becomes the music he dances to as he moves around her. *Click, click, click.* This is the closest to dancing he gets anymore, circling a subject.

He asks her about where she lives and who she lives with and she answers him. Upper Boylston Street, two roommates. She talks about Bobby and Carol, then he asks her about her boyfriend.

There isn't one at the moment, she says. She lets out a sigh, annoyed. Unfortunately.

He seats her by the kitchen table and takes another series of photos, imagining the table is the edge of the piano, beginning to think now of the painting itself, how he might compose it. This is more deliberate, less playful. This is starting to explore some actual possibilities.

Why do you sketch if you use a camera? she says.

I get a different feeling from them. They make me see you in different ways. The drawing's much more physical; the photographs are objective. I try to work between them— between the way the camera says you look and the way my hand wants to describe it. My hand and my arm. My shoulder, my back.

How do you want to describe me, Harry? She is playing at being seductive again.

Very well, he says crisply. He smirks at her. I want to please your mother.

She glances away from him, disgruntled and amused.

He stops for a moment to sip his coffee. They have a good synergy going here now; this is going very well.

So, he says, setting his coffee down. Tell me about your brother.

He can sense her body stiffen; a certain edge creeps into her eyes.

Harry adopts an elaborately casual tone: they're just chatting aimlessly while he works. I guess you used to sit together at the piano a lot?

Yeah, she says tentatively. We used to sing together.

What did you sing?

Pop songs, show tunes. He liked the funny songs.

Oh yeah? says Harry. He was funny?

She laughs a little laugh, in spite of herself. Yeah, she says. He was funny.

Did he, like, tell jokes? Or...?

No. It was more physical comedy. She drifts a moment, remembering. He used to do this thing, this chicken walk...

A chicken walk? says Harry, poising the camera, ready to start again.

Yeah, she says, instinctively responding to the camera, rising up, becoming more animated. He'd tuck his hands up in his armpits and flap his elbows like wings, like this, then he'd get his head moving in and out, then he'd get his whole body moving in and out, and he'd take these big, high-arching steps.... She lowers her arms, laughs again. He'd come into the kitchen when I was having a fight with my mother and do the chicken walk behind her back. No one could ever stay mad for long.

Harry snaps a shot, then moves around and snaps another. So he was sort of a peacemaker?

No, he was just a distraction.

Did he get along with your parents?

He got along with my mother OK, which was more than I could ever do. But my dad was very demanding of him. He had very high standards for Michael. He wanted him to be the best at whatever he did.

Could you turn a little toward the window? He positions her then backs away, studying the angles, pretending to be only casually interested in what she's saying. What did your father demand of him?

Well he drilled him like a sergeant at sports, as a kid. Michael had to be a star. Not just good, but a star. My father insisted on it.

And was he a star?

Oh yeah. He was very driven. During wrestling season he'd get up at 5AM, load on two or three sweat suits, and go out and run five miles. Then he'd go to school and sit in the sauna and sweat some more. He never ate if he had a match the next day, and sometimes he'd even purge to make weight. Then he'd binge at dinner. It was actually kind of sick, like a model. But he was very successful.

He does sound driven, though.

He was. But he did it to please my father more than for himself, I think.

Did the two of you ever fight?

Oh sure. When we were younger.

About what?

I don't know. Our fights never lasted very long. We were always pretty good friends. Michael was my biggest fan.

Harry stops shooting a moment to study the photos he's just taken, and Lindsay drifts off into thought.

He recorded this show I was in once, she says, her voice much quieter. It's almost as if she's talking to herself. It was an assembly at school, I was singing this song in it. It was just a stupid assembly, I don't even remember what it was for, but the choir had to sing and I had a solo. And Michael recorded it, so my parents could hear it later.

She says all this in a gingerly way, the words coming out haltingly. Every time she reaches the end of a phrase, Harry thinks she's going to stop there, but then another thought bubbles up, almost against her will, it seems. He turns to her and just listens.

He sat down in the front row, she says, glancing up at Harry. I remember seeing him sitting there with the recorder in his lap when we filed out onto the stage. I knew he was going to be sitting there—he'd had to get special permission to sit there, instead of sitting with his homeroom—but when I saw him there it made my heart come up in my throat. Just because, I don't know, I was excited. He saw me see him there and he started jerking his head in and out like he was doing the chicken walk and he got me giggling. I wanted to kill him for making me laugh. I was scared I wouldn't be able to sing.

But when the time came for my solo, he went still. He didn't even look at me. He kept his eyes on the recorder and just held the microphone up. He was probably just keeping an eye on the recording level, but it looked like he was praying or something. Or deliberately looking away from me so he wouldn't distract me. I don't know. But I'll never forget that, how he didn't look at me.

She glances at Harry now with a look of wonder in her eyes, wonder and perplexity. That night, she says, when he played the recording at dinner…. We all sat there listening, and it sounded pretty good. It wasn't a very good recording but you could tell I'd done OK. And at the end? When the audience was applauding? He'd whispered into the microphone *That was beautiful, Lindsay.* He just whispered it. *That was beautiful.* She looks up at Harry again, her eyes glittering. That was the best part of the recording.

Harry holds her gaze. It sounds like Michael was a lovely guy.

She nods. He was.

Harry watches her. He is touched in so many ways, just now—by Michael's gesture, by Lindsay's telling, by his own response—it feels to him as if a ghost has just passed through the room. But then he remembers himself, remembers what he's supposed to be doing, gathering images for a painting. And he thinks, *Grab hold of this moment. Capture this moment. This is the subject of this painting. Grab it now, before it passes.* So he raises his camera to shoot again. But the light in Lindsay's eyes disappears. He lowers the camera, startled. But of course the light has disappeared. She must feel the way accident victims feel when the press descends upon them with all their cameras and microphones.

I'm sorry, he says. I'm sorry. He looks at the floor, then up at her. You must have loved your brother very much.

She stares at him, all coldness. Of course I loved my brother, you ass.

She shoots to her feet and stalks away, looking out the window at the traffic on the turnpike. She stands there for a long moment, then finally turns and looks at him. Do you think you have enough now?

I'd like to get some more, he says. He knows better than to think he can actually call that moment back, but he feels he has to try. It's what he's being paid to do. Although, if he's honest with himself—and he will be honest about it, later, looking back on it—in his heart he knows the real reason he is asking her to continue is not so much to try to record that glittering look in her eyes as it is to try to reestablish the intimacy he'd just felt with her. He betrayed her trust, and he needs her to trust him.

Just a few more? he says. By the table?

She stares at him as if she's looking at an errant child. Exasperated, she returns to the table and sits. But she is closed, she is giving him nothing.

Harry leans toward her, elbows on knees, looking up at her like a coach. I'm sorry, he murmurs. I know this is hard. But I felt like I saw in you just now all the feeling you had for Michael, and all the feeling he had for you. And I want that to be what this painting is about. I want to try to capture that.

She makes a face, the face an older sister makes when a younger brother wants to tag along.

Will you tell me some more about Michael?

Harry...

Please? What was he like?

She studies him, her eyes locked on his, daring him to look away. It's disarming, being looked at that way, but he holds her gaze, he can't look away, then finally—he can't help himself—he relaxes and lets her in.

Her gaze seems to widen and deepen. What did my mother tell you about the way my brother died?

She said a hunting accident.

A hunting accident?

Yes.

Her mouth curls up in a rueful smile. She looks up at the ceiling. That's an interesting twist.

Harry cocks his head.

Lindsay shifts her weight. My mother's grasp on reality can be a little...tenuous, one might say. Michael never went hunting in his life.

Then why...?

She looks at him with that same penetrating gaze, then seems to locate some resolve in herself. My brother killed himself, she says.

A chill creeps over Harry's shoulders, his muscles go suddenly slack.

Lindsay watches his reaction, seems satisfied and a little surprised with his expression of shock.

How? he breathes at last.

A gun, she says. She has that part right. But it wasn't an accident. He went out into the woods behind our house and sat on a rock.... She closes her eyes, takes a deep breath. Then he put the gun in his mouth...

Harry's stomach tightens, his throat goes thick. *Why?*

She shrugs. That's the million-dollar question.

He didn't leave a note?

Nothing.

Are you sure it was a suicide?

Now you sound like my mother.

Does she really think it was an accident?

I don't know what she thinks. No. She knows he did it himself. But she doesn't want people to know, she thinks they'll blame her or something. So she insists the public story is that it was an accident. That's what she told everybody, and now I think she's to the point she actually believes it. It's easier to believe that than to think he did it himself.

But don't you have *any* idea why? He seems to have had so much going for him.

She takes a deep breath and leans forward. He had come home for Thanksgiving from Dartmouth. He did it the Sunday he was to go back. I had already left to come back here. He'd seemed OK over the weekend. I guess he did seem a little low, but I figured it was just sophomore slump. I just punched him on the shoulder, told him to buck up. I didn't have any idea...

Did you talk with his friends at school? Or his teachers?

My father did. He went out there. Michael's roommate said that Michael hadn't been able to sleep or study. He wasn't getting his work done, he was going to get a couple of Incompletes, maybe even flunk one course. This would have been a big deal, to Michael. I guess he was out a lot of the time, no one knew where, or what he was doing. He'd gone to a counselor a couple of times but the counselor didn't know anything. He said as far as he could tell, Michael just had a mild generalized depression, nothing to get alarmed about.

God, says Harry. This sounds so out of character for Michael. I mean, from what you've told me.

Yeah. But Michael always had a dark streak in him. Sometimes I've thought his funniness was a way to cover that up. There was a sadness in him that he didn't show to people. He wanted to be the cheerful, happy person he always seemed to be, that people wanted him to be, and I think he used to get mad at himself for this melancholy streak. He'd try to slap himself out of it. Pick yourself up, dust yourself off, it's the way my father taught him. It's the way my father taught us both, both my father and my mother. You just keep going, whistle a happy tune, put on a happy face. I remember him singing that song, then putting on this *rigor mortis* smile, this really awful contorted grin, and staggering around the room like he was trying to pry it off, like it was a mask that was stuck on him and he was trying to pry it off. It was hilarious at the time. But it doesn't seem so funny now.

There is a long moment of silence. Then she looks at him. Do you need any more pictures?

He glances at her, surprised. She is looking straight into him now, and there is a strength and fragility in her eyes, a teetering on the edge, that is exactly what he was looking for. It's the strength she has summoned to tell this story and the fragility it stirs in her. Does he dare put a camera between them just now? He burns the image into his brain, instead. It is better remembered that way.

No, he says. That's enough for today.

She nods, looks down at her lap, then stands.

Would you like more coffee?

I've got to go.

He doesn't want her to go. He wants her to stay and show him that face, that fragility and strength. It feels essential to him, beyond the immediate needs of his task here. But he doesn't know how to say that, and he doesn't know if it's true.

In a way he's got what he needed from her, he's got his images. He's done his research, he's made his sketches. But at the same time he feels a hunger for whatever it is she's just shown him.

He watches her walk to the couch and pick up her bag. She opens it, looks through it, in search of something, it seems, but then she snaps it shut and slings it over her shoulder without taking anything out. She seems tired.

Can I get you anything? he says. You sure you don't want more coffee? Some Kleenex?

No, she says. I'm OK. I've got to be on my way.

Thank you for telling me all that.

There aren't very many people I've told. But I guess... Maybe you need to know that. To do your painting, or something.

I'm sorry to put you through it.

You didn't put me through this, she says, waving him away. Michael did.

She hikes her bag up on her shoulder and extends her hand—an uncharacteristically formal gesture, he thinks. Her arm is straight and long and locked at the shoulder, as if she is trying to hold him at a distance. He doesn't like it, but he understands her need to create a safety zone around her, and he honors it, standing back himself when he reaches to shake her hand.

Her hand is firm and cool. Her jaw is set, her chin is stuck out. She doesn't quite see him when she looks at him. He follows her up the stairs and out into the hall, pushes the button to call the lift for her. It's hardly necessary; she's capable of pushing the button, but he feels like he wants to take care of her in this little way. There's an awkward moment as they wait for the lift to arrive.

I'll still need some shots with a piano, he says, apologetically. She nods. I'll find one.

And if you could...

He doesn't want to say this, particularly right now, but they do have business to conduct and the truth of the matter is it's probably best to swim back to that surface so they can both get a little air.

If you could, he says. He sighs. I'll need someone to stand in for your brother. Someone about his size and build. So I can get a sense of how the two of you looked together, the relative scale of things between you and him and the piano. Do you know somebody who could do that...?

God, he hates asking her this at this moment. To ask her to get a stand-in for her brother, as if he could be replaced with any joker off the street who happened to be the right size and shape. He should have waited, and called her later.

She looks at him with dull alarm, as if she can't quite believe he's asking yet more of her but she's too tired to care anyway. I'm sure I can find somebody, she says.

The lift arrives and she opens the door. She pulls back the gate and steps inside, then turns to look at him.

I guess? She says. I guess it would be best if you didn't tell my mother I told you about Michael.

He nods.

Or I don't know. Maybe you should. Maybe it would help her if she heard it from somebody else. She shakes herself free of the thought. I'll find a piano, she says. And a guy. I'll give you a call in a few days.

I appreciate your cooperation.

She nods and closes the gate. She is clearly not interested in hearing anything more from him now. He stands there stupidly, holding the door. She pushes the button for the lobby but the lift, of course, doesn't move. She looks at him, impatiently. Oh, he says. Sorry. He closes the door and the lift clicks into motion, disappearing downward.

Back in his studio, Harry takes the coffee cups to the kitchen, puts the cookies back in the box, the grapes back in the refrigerator. Then he sits at his computer and reviews the photos he's just taken. He has a couple of dozen, at various angles, in various poses—they will give him what he needs, as reference points—but none of them comes even close to the picture he has of her in his mind, that mix of pain and resolve. It occurs to him to try to sketch it, but he doesn't think he could capture it now. He thinks the most he'd be able to do is destroy the picture in his mind by replacing it with a pale imitation. He knows that once he drew it, the drawing would be what he remembered, not the look in her eyes. So he just studies the image in his mind, allowing his associations to gather around the memory like creatures gathering around a fire, comforted and mesmerized.

5

Lindsay hesitates a moment, then she figures what the hell, she'll wear the pearls too. It's a lesson she learned from auditioning: whenever you get a callback, you wear the same thing you wore the first time. There was something they saw in you they liked—you don't know what it is, but somehow you must have looked the part—so you try to look the same as before. She figures the last time she got together with Harry went so well, she'll dress the same for him this time.

In the few days since that last session, her attitude toward Harry has changed. She still doesn't like the project much, but she feels OK about this painter. It felt good when he got her to talk about Michael. Most people tiptoe around the subject like it's a bomb they're scared of setting off, and she doesn't really invite questions. But once she started talking to Harry about him, she sort of liked it. It was nice to remember that assembly at school. To talk about Michael's chicken walk. Even talking about the suicide. That's something *no one* wants to talk about, not even her parents. Especially her parents. But this guy Harry seemed able to hear it, somehow. He didn't run off scared. He even seemed to understand, in some way.

She steps into her heels, grabs her bag and heads for the door. Bobby is lying on the living room couch reading the paper in his kimono. He glances at her and does a double take. Where you goin all dressed up? She reminds him about the photo session and he lowers the paper. This the thing you asked Curt to help you with?

Yeah.

Ooo, girl, says Bobby. I'd dress for him on a Saturday too.

Lindsay grabs the pillow from under his feet and throws it at him, then slips out the door, a little flustered, hurrying down the stairs. Is Bobby right? Did she dress to impress—for Curt? At least a little? She doesn't know him all that well—he's a year behind her at school—but he *is* very attractive, in a matinee idol kind of way. He'll probably do very well in the soaps. She asked him to stand in for Michael because he's built the same—same height, same weight, same frame—and he even looks a little like Michael looked. His face is more angular and dramatic, more model-like, and his hair has that sexy falling-in-the-eyes thing going, instead of Michael's wavy mop. But there is a resemblance. She doesn't think there's much likelihood of anything happening with Curt. If something were going to happen it would probably have already happened. Still, she'd be *open* to interest from him. She wouldn't be *averse* to it. She could use a little attention. She could use a little loving. What she could use is a good fuck. There is something in that, for sure. Sometimes she feels like all she really needs is just a good fuck.

When she gets to the school, Harry is there, waiting at the front door. He looks sort of scruffy and bleary, like he just got out of bed, but he seems happy to see her. He remarks on how nice she looks, that she needn't have bothered to get dressed up.

But, he says, I'm glad you did.

There seems to be something in that remark, she isn't sure exactly what, but she's glad to see him too. He's wearing sunglasses, a T-shirt and jeans, and a sweatshirt unzipped. It looks like he has a pretty good body. She was right about that.

Not bad for a forty-year-old guy. Or however old he is: she guesses 35 or 40.

They talk about the weather a minute then Curt arrives in shorts and a tank top showing off his shoulders and arms. She told him he didn't need to dress but Christ, he's barely *dressed*. And she can tell by the way Harry looks at him.... It happens in an instant, in the space of time it takes them to shake hands, and it's very subtle, but she picks up on it. She knows too many gay guys not to be able to see these things. Harry is gay. Her initial hunch was right.

They go upstairs to the rehearsal studio and she leaves them there while she goes to the bathroom. She's combing her hair, watching herself in the mirror and thinking she looks pretty good, when she realizes she is pissed off. Very, in fact, pissed off. Two attractive guys and they're interested in each other. Well, she doesn't know if Curt is interested in Harry, but Harry is clearly drawn to Curt and it rankles her. She doesn't care if he's gay, but why did he have to be so coy about it? He doesn't sleep with anyone; he's a monk. He's just a liar, that's all. She throws her brush back in her bag and goes back to the studio, dropping her bag on a chair. OK, she says. Let's do this thing.

With Curt's help, Harry pulls the piano around so the light from the window will fall across from the left, then he turns to Lindsay. Now, he says. Do you use a bench, at home? Or a chair?

A bench, she says. Sort of like this.

OK, says Harry, pulling the bench into place and moving the chairs. Why don't you have a seat here?

Lindsay sits, fans her skirt beside her knees.

And Curt? says Harry. Could you stand...here. He positions Curt behind her; pulls him around by the arm, hands all over him. Then he steps back and looks at the two of them. Michael would come up behind you, right Lindsay? While you were playing?

She nods.

And stand behind you...like this?

She turns and looks up at Curt. He is standing very close. Yeah, she says. Pretty much.

Harry backs away and frames a shot. Would you...? Curt, would you move to the right just a bit? Like that, yes. Lean forward a bit.

He takes a series of pictures, creeping around them like a predator, and Lindsay feels that he's really taking pictures of Curt, not her.

Lindsay, he says. Would he touch you? Would he put his hands on your shoulders sometimes?

Lindsay bristles. Sometimes, yes.

Curt? says Harry. Could you just put one hand on Lindsay's shoulder? Yes, like that. Move your head to the left? Lindsay can feel the heat of Curt's hand on her shoulder and it makes her want to jump out of her skin.

Harry takes another series of photos, then moves to the other side of the piano and takes some more. He asks Curt to sit beside Lindsay on the bench, then moves around behind the piano and shoots them through the triangle formed by the opened lid. He asks Lindsay to move this way and that and she does everything he asks, but with every request he makes she finds herself getting more and more irritated.

Lindsay, says Harry. Why don't you play something?

She closes her eyes to calm herself, then positions herself on the bench and picks out a few chords. Repositions herself, picks out a few more. Then she launches into a Chopin etude, playing it too loud. Harry moves to Curt and silently stands him up, hands all over him again, while Lindsay continues to play. He steps back and takes a photo. Moves around, then takes another.

OK, he says, interrupting her. Lindsay, try playing something else. Try playing one of the songs you sang with Michael.

She looks at him a moment. He is *really* pushing it, here. And he seems to be doing it on purpose. He seems to *want* to make her mad. Or he seems to want *something* out of her. And if he keeps pushing like this he's going to get something, that is for sure. She picks at the keyboard a few times, thinking. Then finally she starts playing a vamp—*oomp-ba-da, oomp-ba-da, oomp-ba-da boom.*

What is that? says Harry. What's the song?

She stops and looks at him. It's a song about *money*, she says, drilling the word right into him. That's what he's all about here, after all—shoveling around in her life, in her heart, just so he can make a buck.

Why don't you sing it? he says.

She stares at him a moment, then stares at him a moment longer, then slams down the keyboard cover. No, she says, standing up. That's it.

Lindsay...

I've had it, Harry. That's all.

He takes a step back, his mouth hanging open.

What the fuck do you want from me? You think you can push me around like I'm a lump of clay or something. Like I'm some laboratory animal you can poke and prod for a response. Well I've had it, Harry. I've fucking had it. I'm not going to sit here and be pushed around by you anymore.

She grabs her bag and turns to Curt. Thanks for coming, she says. I appreciate your help. Then she slams out of the room, leaving the two of them there alone. May they live happily ever after.

Harry looks at Curt, dumbfounded and embarrassed.

This is kind of hard for her, says Curt. I mean, her brother is *dead*.

I know, sighs Harry. I know. He sets his camera on the piano, then closes his eyes and shakes his head, placing his fingers on his temples as if he had a sudden headache, or were trying to receive a telepathic message. After a moment, he looks up at Curt. Thanks, he says, absently. Thanks for your help.

No problem.

Harry nods, distracted. I appreciate it.

Like I said, no problem. Take care of yourself.

Then Curt is out the door and Harry is alone. He looks around the room, confused. It was so full of music just a moment ago and now it's just bare surfaces, and a dim gold light falling through the window, waning September light. He stares out the window at the fire escape, the black-black stripes of the railing against the blond bricks across the alley. The sun-yellow leaves dangling off the black branch angling in from the side. In the distance, he can hear a soprano in another studio singing an aria. She stops in the middle of a phrase, there is talking, then she begins again.

Harry sits at the piano and props his elbows on it, covering his face with his hands. What did he think he was doing, pushing her that way? What was he trying to get from her? He was so pleased when she showed up today, he was a little surprised at how pleased. He saw that she had prepared herself for this session, wearing that same black dress and combing her hair the same as before, even though he'd told her on the phone that wouldn't be necessary.

But when she came back from the bathroom, there was that note of impatience in her voice that unsettled him a bit.

He tried to catch her eye, to lock in a gaze of intention with her, an acknowledgment of the mutual effort they were about to embark upon—and, maybe more importantly, of the place they'd arrived at together, last time—but she wouldn't give him that. It was as if she had never told him all that stuff about Michael last time, as if the two of them hadn't achieved any intimacy at all. And it made him want to push her, to move her back to where they were before. But what did he achieve? He chased her out the door.

He sits back, slumps and studies his hands, scratching green paint off his fingernail, and feels it come over him again—the weight, the flatness, the hollow depth, the unwillingness to move. It will never leave him alone, he thinks. It will never leave him alone. He lifts his fingers to his nose and inhales the faint odor of linseed oil, and it brings him back to himself. He has to paint, that's all. He just has to paint. He reaches for his camera and searches through the pictures he took, looking for one particular shot. There was one in which the play between Lindsay and Curt.... The way Curt bent over her when she was playing the Chopin. The way he seemed to be floating above her, as if he were watching over her, as if he were an angel, or a spirit of some kind. A little smile on his lips. Harry shuffles through the images and finally finds what he's looking for. It is there. It shows the positions and the light, but it doesn't show the idea.

Suddenly energized, Harry reaches for his sketchbook but before he's pulled it out of his bag, he puts it back in and pops the camera in after it. It's far too beautiful a day to sit inside and sketch. He slings the bag over his shoulder, takes a quick look around to be sure he hasn't left anything, then pulls the door shut and heads out. He strides up Hemenway to Boylston and heads off toward Newbury Street to find a café and have a little something while he sketches out his idea. He sets off with purpose, with speed, in defiance of that downward pull that threatened to overtake him just now. He will paint a picture, a beautiful picture, a picture that captures the enduring bond between these two children, and maybe Lindsay will forgive him.

At Ciao Bella, he lucks into a sidewalk table under the trees. He orders a salad and a glass of wine, then pulls out his sketchpad and starts to work out how these figures might fit into a square format. Lindsay seated, looking at the viewer. Michael behind her, reaching out to touch her shoulder. Like a spirit watching over her, a presence protecting her. It will all, of course, be subtext. It will all be only suggestion. On the surface, it will appear to be only two people at a piano. But the feeling it gives will be something different, the sense of peace it gives will be mysterious and subtle. And, Harry hopes, maybe healing. He likes the way this looks. He's starting to feel downright optimistic. It's hard to imagine just moments ago he was feeling so lost and alone.

The waiter brings the wine and Harry notices his hands, and the rings—two rings on his middle finger, another on his thumb. He has his sleeves rolled up to his elbows; his forearms are beautifully veined and muscled, like something from a Bernini sculpture. He looks up at the boy—a man, in fact, but everyone under thirty looks like a boy these days—and takes in the stubbled chin, the warm bright eyes.

The waiter looks over his shoulder at the sketchbook. Nice, he murmurs, his hands on his hips.

Oh, says Harry. It's just a sketch.

I like it, says the waiter. You're good.

Harry glances down at the page like a parent admiring his child. It's just a sketch for a painting, he says.

Ah, says the waiter. You're a painter.

I am.

What kind of stuff do you paint? He seems to be genuinely interested.

People, says Harry simply, looking up at him. He really does have beautiful eyes.

People, repeats the waiter, as if he finds some special meaning in that. Do you paint as well as you draw?

Harry shrugs and smiles. Hope so.

The waiter considers him a moment. What's going on behind those eyes? I'll bet you do, he says at last. Then he disappears.

Harry sits still for a moment, wondering what that was, that just happened. Then he shakes it off and continues sketching until he is satisfied that he has captured his idea before it could abandon him, floating blithely off into the ether, smug and indifferent. Now he can relax. He has found what he needs and has claimed it as his.

He sets his pad aside and settles back with his drink. This is one of his favorite activities, sitting in a sidewalk café watching the world pass by. Sometimes he makes up stories about the people passing by—wondering who they are, where they're going and why—but mostly he just watches them like fish in an aquarium, allowing himself to be mesmerized by their color and movement, allowing himself to be hooked by any human fish that happens by and dragged a while in its wake.

Today, as he watches, he wonders if any of them are Lindsay's friends. Many of them seem about her age. Is this where she fits in the larger world? Is this where she hangs out? Might he actually see her here? He has only seen her so far in studio spaces and, except for that first day, only dressed in clothes she doesn't usually wear. What does she look like, usually? What kind of people does she spend time with? Guys like Curt? he wonders. And what about Curt? Are all her friends that hot?

The waiter brings his salad and sets it in front of him. With those arms, with those hands. Harry looks up at the smile, at the eyes, and feels a glitch in his throat.

Can I get you anything else? the waiter wants to know, eyes bright with interest. Harry looks up, interested himself.

I don't know, he hears himself saying. You got any suggestions?

Whatever you want, says the boy, lighting up.

Well, Harry says. I'll give that some thought.

OK, says the waiter calmly, placing a hand on Harry's shoulder. Think about it. Then give me a holler.

Harry nods, then watches after him as he wanders back to the waiters' station and chucks a wad of paper into a wastebasket, like a basketball.

Harry turns to his salad, slightly disoriented. It has been a while since he's engaged in this kind of play with a stranger. It has been a while since he's engaged in any kind of flirtation at all and it feels odd, like an old suit of clothes that doesn't fit quite right anymore. It feels odd, but also oddly fun. He doesn't expect this kind of response from himself much anymore, being the monk he has become. When he has felt that little surge of interest, that little quickening in the throat, that magnetic pull, he has turned away from it, with purpose. But here today, with this waiter, feels different. Is it the waiter himself who makes the difference? Is it his juxtaposition with Curt? Of Curt with Lindsay? Is it the elation of having just hit on the right idea for this painting, a generalizing of that excitement? Whatever it is, it makes him giddy. His appetite is suddenly gone. He orders another glass of wine and when the waiter brings it, tells him he can take the salad.

Is there anything wrong? he says. He bends over when he says it, as if he is saying something intimate.

Oh, says Harry. No. I'm just not very hungry. For salad.

Oh, says the waiter. Well. Is there anything else you'd like? Again those warm eyes. Again those arms, those hands.

Harry turns to him. Yes, he says. Yes. I think I'd like to paint you.

Paint me?

Yes, says Harry. I think so.

The waiter cocks his weight on one hip. I could be into that, he says. I've done some modeling. For photographers. You know.

Ah, says Harry dismissively. Photographers. Slaves to reality.

You like to get a little...wild? With the paint?

Well, I don't know if you'd call me wild, but I like to play around a bit, yes. He reaches into his bag. Why don't I give you my card....

The waiter takes the card, turns it over. Harry Garrett, he reads aloud. He looks back at Harry. My name is Patrick.

Give me a call sometime, Patrick.

Yeah, says Patrick. Maybe I will.

I'm just up the street.

The waiter looks at the card again, nodding, then slips it in his back pocket. Just a sec, he says. I'll get your check.

Harry sits back and sips his wine. He feels ruffled inside, vaguely celebratory. When Patrick returns with the check, Harry pays him on the spot, rounding up for a generous tip.

Thanks, Patrick chirps. I'll call you.

Do that, says Harry, standing. He holds out his hand and the waiter shakes it. You do have interesting eyes, says Harry.

The waiter fixes his eyes on Harry, warm and dark and amused. The rest of me's not bad either, he says.

The radio is on when Harry comes into his studio—he leaves it on, to welcome him home—and as he walks in he hears piano jazz and a friendly murmuring voice. He locks the door, then checks his voicemail. There is just one message, from Gillian, who wants him to come out to Concord to see her new studio.

You need to get out of town anyway, she says. You've been staring at that turnpike too long.

Harry jots her name down and vows to call her back, but for now he just wants to contemplate this project he's embarking upon. He gets himself a Corona and collapses on the couch, propping his feet on the steamer trunk, the bottle angled on his thigh, and stares across the room at the blank white canvas he stretched yesterday.

He loves this moment in the process maybe most of all, the moment before he has made a mark, when everything is still yet-to-be, when perfection is still a possibility. After this it's all compromise between what he can see and what he can do. But in this moment, the promise is incandescent. Everything past has been erased. Everything future is yet to be. It's a moment of perfect poise, like a diver at the edge of the platform. A moment of perfect stillness and balance, perfect readiness. And then the slight tilting, the pushing off, the falling through the air, falling through space and time and trusting that he will know what to do.

He takes a swig of his beer and feels his day come coursing through him again. Lindsay and Curt. Lindsay storming out.

That waiter, his arms, his hands, his eyes. He feels all those moments gather in him as if they've been called to a conference, and feels them begin to turn into something else, something that shimmers like a column of light inside him, turning *him* into something else.

In a few moments he will finish his beer, then get up and go about his business. He'll scan the sketches he made today and send them to Marjorie Davenport with an explanation of his plans. He'll return the call to Gillian and make a date to see her. He'll finish an article in last Sunday's *New York Times Magazine* and even watch a little television. But all the time he is doing those things, in reality he will still be here staring at this blank white space, feeling the light coalesce inside him.

And when, at 3AM, he awakes to the sound of someone calling his name—a man's voice, as clear and real as if he is standing just outside Harry's door *(Harry!)*—Harry will get out of bed and pad out to his kitchen to see what that sound could have possibly been. And finding nothing in his kitchen, he'll wander out to his studio, where he'll come upon this canvas again, seeming to float on its easel in the darkness like a ghost, glowing in the half light from the vapor lamps on the turnpike outside, a five-foot square of luminescent possibility. And Harry will stand there naked, wondering who it was that called his name.

PART II

6

David sees them when he walks in but he takes a seat at the end of the bar in hopes they won't see him. He's not in the mood for people just now; he just wants to have his scotch, or maybe two, then be on his way.

He's always been the kind of guy who finds it hard to leave the office, but lately it's gotten still harder to muster the will to head back home. At the end of the day he's exhausted from holding up through all the meetings and phone calls, and home, rather than a haven from that, has come to feel like yet another demand, another place where he has to train his attention and focus his energies on something he'd really rather not think about. All he wants to do is stare at a wall, or better yet a TV screen, and let his mind let go, exactly the kind of TV watching he used to criticize Michael for.

He orders the scotch from the bartender—it's the same bartender every day but David has not learned his name, and doesn't want to—then hunches over it for that first sharp sip before settling back to watch the news. But he's barely slipped his canoe into the current when he feels the slap on his back.

David! Old man! Come join us!

It's Clint, from marketing. An important ally, an occasional golfing friend, a friendly eager face—exactly what David doesn't want right now.

Clint, sighs David wearily. Buddy, I'm kind of tired tonight.

Come on, he says. I want you to meet a new member of our team.

David glances over at the table in the far corner. Two other guys from marketing and a new girl, youngish, attractive.

Oh, he sighs. All right. He grabs his scotch and slides off his stool.

When Clint introduces the girl—her name is Charlene—David notices something in her air. She is attractive, friendly, but there is something hard-bitten about her. A weariness, a faintly red-tinged glaze to her eyes. He notices it, he doesn't know if the others do. It makes him think she's been through something.

He slides in across from her and turns his attention to the office talk, the same sort of stuff he's been forcing himself to listen to all day. Sales figures. Competitive branding. While they're talking, Charlene's cell phone rings—a simple buzz, no songs, no clever tones—and she fishes in her bag to find it. She pulls out a book and sets it on the table as she rummages. Finally she locates the phone and flips it open to see who's calling. When she sees who it is, she closes the phone again and tucks it back into her bag, her lips a little more tightly compressed, then reaches for her glass. David watches her, sure that he understands something about her from that. It is something that makes him smile from some dark place within him. He watches her intently and he knows that she knows he's watching. It is only the slightest moment, over in an instant, but it has happened.

This is quite a title, he says, nudging the book with his knuckle. *Because It Is Bitter,* he reads aloud, *and Because It Is My Heart.*

She arches a brow and nods. It's quite a book.

What's it about?

Murder, mayhem, racism. Alcoholism, drugs, gambling, All in a broken-down industrial town in upstate New York.

Sounds cheerful.

She shrugs. It's her usual fare. I'm the only person I know who ever reads her stuff.

David nods, watching her intently. You're kind of different, he says.

Yeah, she says, putting the book away. Well, I'm not from around here.

Where are you from?

She laughs. Upstate New York. A little broken-down town out in the middle of nowhere.

David laughs with her and they launch into more conventional fare: what first brought her to Ohio, what her new job is at P&G, what part of town she lives in.

Mount Lookout, she says. I've recently become a career girl again.

Ah, says David, nodding as if he already knew that.

They turn their attention to the table again—the topic now is the Bengals and their prospects for the season—but all the while they talk, David is aware of this woman beside him, aware of what he takes to be her fierce determination—*Because It Is Bitter and Because It Is My Heart*—and it makes him feel emboldened somehow. Quickened, alert, like a dog that has caught a scent.

He notices her hands, fiddling with her cocktail napkin, folding it, then folding it, then folding it again. He notes the pallor of her skin, the length of her legs crossed at the knee just under the table. He listens to her banter with the others about the football team, notes the attentiveness of her gaze as she listens, willing herself to be interested.

When she excuses herself for the ladies' room, David turns to Clint, who is watching him for a reaction. He doesn't give Clint any reaction at all, just stares back at him blankly. As if to say, What are you looking at? It feels a little strange for him to react like that, it feels like a mild form of betrayal. He understands that Clint is looking for some sort of agreement about this woman, but David is not sure that he and Clint are in agreement on her. David is not sure that Clint understands what David has understood. David's not sure he understands it himself.

When the group breaks up, David takes the long way home, along the river, up through Mariemont, enjoying the rush of the warm late summer air and the sounds of Neil Young on the CD player. These are roads he has traveled countless times at all times of day, in all kinds of weather, in all different states of mind. But tonight it seems like an adventure, as if he can't be absolutely sure what he'll find around the next curve. He likes this unfamiliarity, this attention to the moment, and drives as if he's driving the MG, quickly, sharply, sporty. An elbow out the window, one hand grasping the wheel, a close attention to the road. It all feels very alive, Right Now. Sure and sharply drawn. There is no room for error.

As he draws closer to home, he is increasingly aware of wanting to extend this feeling, to keep himself on this roll. But there is really no place to go except home—driving aimlessly would not work; driving aimlessly would put him right back where he doesn't want to be—so when he comes upon the high school he takes a quick turn in, on impulse.

He parks near the football field and climbs into the bleachers to watch the team practice. It's a beautiful summer evening, the boys are fully suited up, running in place, falling, rising, shouting in unison. He doesn't know the boys this year but there is a certain comfort in this scene, a certain familiarity. It does seem a little dangerous to be here at Michael's high school, but he feels up to danger just now.

He listens to the sounds of shoulder pads colliding, the boys' grunts and heavy breathing, the called instructions from the coaches. It calls back layers and layers of summer evenings just like this one when he was out on the gridiron himself, at practice, and it feels to him as if it puts him in touch with who he used to be. Young and full of energy. Cocky, full of swagger. His whole life laid out before him, waiting. Mountains to climb. Rivers to cross. Triumphs to be catalogued. It all comes back to him like a vague scent, a wisp of smoke from burning leaves, a smell you never smell anymore: rich and aromatic, pungent and sweet.

He is settling in to this sweet nostalgia when he hears his name called out. He looks to the edge of the bleachers and sees Frank...what is his name? Frank Dawson, Michael's old wrestling coach, climbing the risers to greet him.

David stands and shakes the man's hand. How are things going? he says. Your team going to have a good season?

Yeah, says Frank. We've got a pretty good group this year. Got a receiver out already though, with a shoulder separation. That's gonna hurt us. But I think we're looking at a pretty good season.

They stand there and talk for maybe ten minutes about the team's prospects, where their strengths are, their weaknesses, what the competition looks like. None of it is of any real interest to David, it's all just a script to run through, the same conversation he might have with anybody. Except this man is not anybody. This man was Michael's coach. He was, in a distant way, an ally of David's, a man he entrusted his son to.

A man who cared about him, shared responsibility for him. And here they are talking like two strangers who never had anything in common. How can this man stand here talking football when he knows that Michael is gone? How can he not mention it? Not offer his condolences? His regrets? His bafflement? His horror? How can he just carry on as if nothing has happened to David?

But he does. The conversation comes and goes without any mention of Michael at all. Played entirely by the book, no deviations from the script, a conversational box that they entered and did not leave until Frank made his way back down the bleachers and out again to the playing field.

David is furious that this man could ignore what was standing right between them. It is a profoundly insulting thing. But at the same time, he is grateful for this *pro forma* encounter. Grateful that he wasn't forced to broach that subject again, with a stranger. Grateful to pretend, for a moment, that Michael isn't gone. He can't endure these two feelings at once, the outrage and the gratitude. It's like he's two people. What in hell does he want? Is there *any* encounter that would satisfy him?

He picks himself up and heads back to his car. He has to get away from this place, these memories, Michael's school. Why did he ever come here? He is disgusted with himself, disgusted with the disarray in him. Ashamed and hurt and angry, angry. Angry at Dawson. At himself. At this day, this month, this year. At Michael. It is a mess, *he* is a mess. Nothing makes any sense anymore. He climbs into his car, spits gravel as he backs out of the space, and hurries out of the parking lot, heading home to Marjorie.

7

At eleven, Lindsay and Bobby go out to shoot pool. It is a beautiful Indian Summer night, much too warm to stay indoors the whole time. They've both been aware, as they've studied, of people passing by on the street outside, walking their dogs, stopping to chat, heading toward the clubs. They've both been aware of the fragrance of the night, that soft summer smell laced with autumn spice, and it's made them both want to move, to get up, get out, get going. They are young, they are in the city, it's night. They grab their cigarettes and go.

They walk around the corner to a bar Bobby likes, called Machine—upstairs it's dark and black leather, downstairs it's pool and dancing—but all the tables are taken tonight, so they continue up to Kilmarnock Street and duck into The Linwood Grill. Small and funky, a very different crowd. They get themselves a table and a couple of beers, start circling the felt like animals on the veldt circling their prey. They chalk their cue sticks and study their shots, then lay their cigarettes carefully on the edge of the table—hanging over the edge, sending up curls of smoke like little campfires—point confidently with their sticks, then crouch into position and shoot.

Lindsay loves this process, strutting around the table, chalking her cue. It feels like a male prerogative to survey a situation like this, to point with a stick as if with a scepter, to assess her options, make her choices. She likes it. She likes the feeling of being in control like this. She takes a long pull on her beer and looks around the room, surveying the situation, and notices, by the bar, a guy is watching her. She plants her bottle on the table, stalks another shot, stretching her back out a little longer this time when she bends to shoot. She sinks one, stands, circles, surveys. Points, chalks, bends, stretches. Sinks another. Does it again, but on the third shot misses.

She curses and stands back, cocking her weight on one hip, holding her cue stick like a flagstaff, taking another pull off her beer, then cuts her eyes again to the guy by the bar. Still watching. Tall, dark, good-looking. Skinny. A kind of a porkpie hat and a scraggly goatee. She sets down her beer, runs her fingers through her hair, breathes deep and shakes her hair out.

Bobby is on a roll. One in the corner, two on the side, three in the corner, four. Read 'em and weep, he says, chalking up his cue.

That's cards, says Lindsay dryly.

Details, he says, waving her away. Then he finishes off the game, sinking the eight ball in the corner pocket.

Want another beer? Lindsay says. You rack 'em up, I'll get this round.

He sets about his business and she makes her way through the crowd, angling into a space at the bar just a few stops down from her admirer. She glances at him as she orders and he is still watching her, smiling, nodding. He *is* sort of cute, she thinks. In fact, she thinks, he is very cute.

She feels herself click into a lower gear, rolls her shoulders a little, then glances back at the guy and sees he is moving toward her. She feels her throat clutch; she straightens. He wedges into the space beside her.

Wanna buy me a beer? he says, smiling.

She gives him a sideways glance. That's the first time I've heard that opener.

He shrugs and smiles disarmingly. I see you already have your own.

Yeah, she says. And one for my friend.

You with him? he says. Very direct.

I'm with him tonight.

Can I give you a call?

She studies him. He has beautiful eyes, lashes luxurious as mink. I don't even know your name.

Aldo, he says. What's yours?

She considers him a moment more. Lindsay.

Lindsay.

She nods.

Well Lindsay, he says. I'd like to know you.

She studies him a long moment. He stands there, willing to be studied. He doesn't seem to feel the need to rush in with a lot of words, he's willing to just present himself and let her make her choice. Although she imagines, if she said no, he wouldn't leave it there.

I don't have a pen, she says at last.

I can fix that. He leans across the bar, gets the bartender's attention fast, gets a pen and a cocktail napkin. Very competent. He places them on the bar in front of her, then leans back to watch her write. He watches her as if he thinks she's going to draw a picture or something.

She picks up the pen and starts to write her number. She writes it slowly, wondering with each digit whether she will scramble the number or write it out accurately. Will she give him access, or not? He is a total stranger. He could be a serial murderer. Eight ball in the corner pocket. She writes it right, sets down the pen, picks up her beers to go.

This the right number, Lindsay?

She turns to look at him. You'll have to call to find out, she says. Then she moves abruptly away, secretly giddy and flustered.

Don't look now, she says to Bobby when she gets back to the table. But you see that guy over by the bar? The tall guy with the goatee, in the T-shirt? With the hat?

What do you mean, Don't Look Now? Bobby says. How can I see him if I Don't Look Now? He circles the table, chalking his cue, and glances up at the bar. That Latin guy? he says, as he bends to line up his shot. She nods. Ooo darlin, he says. *Muy macho. Muy atractivo.*

I just gave him my phone number.

Bobby breaks the balls and straightens again, arching his brows and turning down the corners of his mouth as if to say Aren't we the tramp? None of the balls go in. He glances at the guy again. Well, he says, if you're not home when he calls, I'll take care of him.

Lindsay punches him in the shoulder then holds her beer up to her mouth, swaying her back like a little girl holding a lollipop. She feels oddly out of body now. As much as she felt sunk into her bones just moments ago, now she feels as if she's been hollowed out, like an Easter egg. It isn't an unpleasant feeling, exactly, but it feels insubstantial, fragile. And when she glances at the bar again, that guy Aldo is gone.

She plays another game with Bobby, but she's distracted and doesn't play well. And by now it's late; there's school tomorrow, so they make their way to the door. As they leave, she locates Aldo leaning against the wall, looking in the other direction. She wants to go talk to him, or parade in front of him, to get his attention again somehow. She wants to get his attention and then ignore him, walk out on him, laughing. She wants him to want her, then she wants to turn her back on him. But he is looking the other way.

So you think your Ricky Martin will call? says Bobby, when they are out on the street.

Beats me, she shrugs, giving the impression she doesn't care.

But when she gets back to her room, she lies in bed and gazes up at the shadows the streetlights cast on her ceiling, streamlined shadows of trees and power lines, blurred as if they're in motion.

Why does she feel so unsettled? So scared? She's given out her phone number to guys in bars before. A thousand girls do it every night. But usually she's done it only after she's talked with a guy for a while, usually only if he knows somebody else in her group.

She stares into the shadow in the corner of her room, imagines someone crouching there, watching her from the dark, and feels a chill run through her. A number is just a number, she tells herself. He doesn't know where she lives. He doesn't know her last name. She can always pretend she never heard of a Lindsay, if he calls.

But when she remembers the feel of his eyes on her, and the way he leaned back to watch her write out her number, she doesn't think she'll do that.

8

When Harry arrives at Ciao Bella for lunch, Gillian is already seated at a table on the sidewalk. She waves to get his attention and he picks his way through the tables to her.

Hello dahling, she says, extending an arm to him and emphasizing her South African accent in a way she knows he likes. Where have you *bean?* I've bean desperate for you.

I'm only three minutes late, he says, kissing her on the cheek. Her hair is wiry; she smells of coconut. God I love how you smell, he says. It reminds me of suntan lotion. Makes me feel like I'm at the beach.

Yes, she smirks. Well that's me. I'm just a day at the beach.

He takes the seat across from her. She is dressed, as usual, in jeans and a jersey top with a sheer purple scarf tied loosely around her neck, only the slightest hint of make-up. Her skin seems to glow, like alabaster.

So how did your meeting go? he asks.

Oh fine, she sings, waving a hand. She's going to hang five of my pictures. The black-and-whites of the fishermen? It should be a very good show. She goes on to talk about the show and the other photographers in it, and the gossip she heard about one of them with another's boyfriend. Then she asks him how he's doing.

Oh, he says, glancing around to see if that waiter, Patrick, is here. I'm OK, I guess. I've started that new painting.

The one of the girl and her brother?

He nods.

So how's it going?

Well it *has* been going really well, he says. He snaps his napkin open and spreads it on his lap. I mean, I'm loving the composition. And the figures are coming along really well. Especially Lindsay, the girl. There's this really interesting ambiguity to her. But…. He adjusts his silverware. I'm having some trouble with Michael.

A waitress arrives to take their drink order. Harry is a little disappointed that it's not Patrick, and a little relieved. They order their drinks and their lunch all at once, so as not to be interrupted too much, then settle back in their chairs.

So what's the problem with the boy? says Gillian.

I can't put my finger on it, says Harry. Technically everything looks OK—you know, I got the *nose* in the right place—but somehow he doesn't feel right. I've been sitting with it all morning. You know, like you sit with a sick friend, waiting for them to get better? I just sat there and stared at it for two hours. But I still don't know what's wrong.

Maybe you should do something else for a while.

Well that's what I did. I came to have lunch with you. Maybe by the time I get home he'll have worked it out for himself.

The waitress brings their food, asks if they'd like anything more, then moves away. As they begin to eat, Patrick the waiter stops by their table. Hey, he says. How's it going?

Harry looks up, startled.

The painter, right? Harry. Right?

Yeah, says Harry, a little flustered.

Patrick, says the waiter, placing his hand on his chest. Harry notices the rings again, and the veined forearms.

Yeah, says Harry. I remember.

Patrick grins and nods at him, holding his gaze. So, he says at last, including Gillian. Everything OK here? You need anything?

No, says Harry. We're fine.

OK, says Patrick, still nodding. Well…Good to see you.

Same, says Harry. See you again.

You just might, says Patrick, patting Harry's shoulder and moving off.

Harry stares at his salad, blushing.

Well, sings Gillian. Who was *that?*

Harry glances up at her sheepishly. Just someone I met the other day. He stuffs a tomato into his mouth, straightens up and glances away.

Very cute, says Gillian. A tad on the young side, but very cute.

Harry swallows, a little too hard.

Where did you meet him?

Here, says Harry. He waited on me.

You certainly seem to have hit it off.

Well, says Harry, blushing again. I left him a pretty good tip.

Gillian eyes him wryly.

Harry coughs. And I gave him my card.

How bold.

Isn't it.

Gillian cocks her head. Is Harry possibly getting ready to come out of retirement?

Harry considers her a moment, suddenly without humor, then shrugs. I don't know.

Well it's time you did, you know. You can't stay locked up alone in your studio for the rest of your life.

Oh, he says. I could.

Yeah, she says. You could. She gives him a weary smile. Then she looks across the café and grins slyly. He really is awfully cute, she says.

Harry follows her gaze in time to see Patrick jog up the stairs to the kitchen. Well, he says. We'll see.

9

Marjorie pours herself a mug of coffee, then stands at the kitchen sink a moment, gazing out the window at the trees in the woods out back, all ruby, russet and gold. She picks up her mug with both hands, blowing on the coffee to cool it, closes her eyes as she takes a sip. Then with resolve she goes to the table, picks up the phone and dials. On the sixth ring Lindsay picks up.

Hi Darling! Marjorie chirps. Are you busy?

No, Lindsay mumbles. I just got up.

Oh, says Marjorie. Did I wake you? I'm sorry. I thought you'd be up. It's almost noon.

That's OK.

Were you out late?

Not too, says Lindsay, coming to. But I got incredibly drunk.

Lindsay! says Marjorie. *Why?*

Don't know. Felt like it, I guess.

Lindsay, says Marjorie, all concern. You shouldn't—

I'm just kidding, says Lindsay, cutting off the lecture. I only had a couple of beers.

Oh, says Marjorie. Really?

What's up?

Marjorie repositions herself. Why does Lindsay have to play these games? She's hung over, she's not hung over. Why does she have to toy with her mother that way? Is it some sort of combat? Marjorie doesn't understand, so she just tries to slide by it, tries not to rise to the bait, if bait is what it is. I just wanted to say hello, she says. To see how you're doing.

I'm OK, says Lindsay. Except for this hangover.

Marjorie ignores that. How are rehearsals going?

OK, she says. How are things with you?

Oh, says Marjorie, we're OK. The house seems quiet without you.

And in that moment, she hears it again, in her voice. She never knows when it's going to happen, but sometimes it suddenly takes on layers and layers of overtones, all of them minor, creaking. It's as if a door opens up in her voice revealing a vast expanse of tundra, a cold north wind blowing over it, an endless, boundless howling. And she knows that nothing will drive her daughter farther away, and faster.

But! she says, zipping her voice shut again. I didn't call to talk about that!

Mmmm, says Lindsay. So.... What's up?

Well I just want to talk with you! I want to hear how rehearsals are going! We're so excited about this play, we've been talking it up to everyone here. Your aunt and uncle are going to come see you!

Oh, says Lindsay. That's nice.

Well aren't you *excited* about it? Everyone *else* is! It's such a wonderful opportunity! Have they fit your costumes yet? How many changes do you have?

No. I don't know. A few.

How's the Spanish accent coming?

Pretty good, I guess. Listen, Mom? I'm supposed to meet this guy for coffee in half an hour, so I guess I'd better go pop in the shower.

Oh? says Marjorie. Anyone I know?

I don't even know him. I just met him the other night.

Is he rich? She means it as a joke but Lindsay is not amused.

I have no idea, she says coldly.

Oh, says Marjorie. Then, brightening. Well, what's his name?

Aldo. Listen, I ought to get ready…

Well, I didn't mean to keep you.

You didn't—

I didn't realize—

It's OK—

You didn't tell me—

It's *OK*. But I really do have to get in the shower. Tell Daddy I said hi, OK?

I will. And give us a call sometime? I know he'd like to hear from you.

OK. I'll call.

You mean it?

I'll call. Take care.

I love you, says Marjorie.

Lindsay misses a beat. Me too.

When she hangs up, Marjorie wraps her hands around her coffee mug and lifts it, staring down into the dark liquid. She presses its warm edge to her lips, remembering those afternoons when she would pick Lindsay up from grade school and take her out for a picnic lunch on the golf course across the street. Sometimes she'd pick a dandelion and rub it under Lindsay's chin. If it makes your chin yellow, she would say, then I know you like butter. It always made Lindsay giggle.

She takes a sip of her coffee, listening to the creak of the house, the tick of the clock, all so far away. She pushes herself to her feet and puts her mug back in the sink, and gazes out the window again at the woods in back. It would be a beautiful day, she thinks, for a walk in a woods. She lingers there a moment, dreaming, then feels a curdling in her stomach and turns abruptly away, unsure of where to go or what to do next.

10

This guy Aldo is a problem.

Lindsay took care to be late for their date so she could make an entrance—she isn't a theater major for nothing—but Aldo is even later, so now she's sitting alone with nothing to do but think about the things she learned about him when he called. He is a student at Mass Art, in 3-D, a second-semester junior. He grew up in New Jersey. He's not involved with anyone; he has had relationships before; he isn't on the rebound. He only goes to the Linwood sometimes—he prefers TT's and The Middle East—and he's into ska and punk. The Skatellites, Bim Skala Bim, The Pietasters, dub reggae. This is music that Lindsay has absolutely no connection with, but she liked the energy in his voice—and the way he spiced the conversation with Spanish, Italian and Yiddish—so after talking with him for an hour, she felt OK about seeing him.

But how will I know you? she said. I'm not sure I remember what you look like. It was a lie, of course, but she thought it would be a good tactic.

I'll be the handsome one, he said.

So, he says now, standing over her, grinning. Wanna buy me a cup of coffee?

She looks up at him, narrows her eyes. No, she says. I'm not buying.

Well then, he says. Allow me.

He asks what she wants, then disappears and brings it back to the table with an extra biscotti for her. She takes it as a peace offering, an apology for being late, and maybe for his stupid opener, but he doesn't apologize for either. He sits in the chair across from her, knees spread wide, and leans back. He is cute, she thinks. But he's arrogant.

So how you been? he says. You look nice.

She is wearing a clingy jersey top with a deep scoop neck, showing plenty of cleavage.

Aren't you cold? he says.

She leans forward on the table toward him, her arms folded beneath her breasts, offering him a front row seat. Nothing a little coffee won't help, she says, smirking at his attempt to keep from staring at her breasts. It can be so easy to manage a guy. If he gained a little edge on her by showing up later than she did, she's more than evened the playing field now simply by leaning forward. So now she leans back, and he leans forward.

You do OK on your test? he says.

For a moment she has to scramble to remember what he's referring to—the lie she told about having to study, the night he called. Aced it, she says. *No problema.*

Mazeltov.

She nods her acknowledgment. So where have you been? she says, hoping maybe he'll explain why he's kept her waiting.

I was working in the studio. I've got this great piece going...

He tells her about the sculpture—a big thing, eight feet tall or so and maybe six feet around, an assembly, as near as she can tell, of wood and papier maché: it sounds a little like a homecoming float. He draws her a sketch of it on a napkin and while she can't make much of the drawing, she does like the way he sketches—fast and messy, sure-handed.

She asks him questions to draw him out and as he talks, she finds herself feeling more and more attracted to him. Her questions feed his sense of himself and he puffs up right before her eyes, a swagger in his shoulders. It is wonderful to see, and it makes her feel powerful. But after a while, as he goes on— and on, and on, and on—she begins to feel that she doesn't really even need to be there, he could be talking to himself.

So what kind of girls do you like? she says, a total non sequitur.

He continues sketching for a moment. Different kinds, he says at last, finally looking up at her.

He does have beautiful eyelashes. She leans across the table again, cradling her breasts again. Do you like me?

Yeah, I like you, Lindsay.

She smirks. How much?

He considers her a moment. I bought you a coffee, didn't I?

She turns and squints into the distance, reading the sign behind the counter. Three, four—maybe four dollars' worth.

He shrugs. It's a start.

She sits back, playing at feeling deflated.

Do you like me? he says.

I'm not sure. You're sort of interesting. But I don't like the hat.

You don't like my hat? He removes it. The hat can go, he says.

What else can go?

He looks down at himself, then spreads his arms, helpless. He shakes his head and snorts. My shoes. You like my shoes? He holds one foot up in the air.

She observes the shoe. It's OK, she says.

Oh good, he mutters. She likes my shoes.

What about your virginity?

Huh?

Can you give up your virginity?

This is really new territory for her. She has played around with guys before, playing this sexual teasing game, but this has a new edge to it. This feels more like being some sort of sexual predator. She has never behaved quite like this before, but she wants to try it out. And this guy seems like the guy to try it on. He's too self-absorbed for anything else. May as well use him as a subject for this experiment.

My virginity? he says. What makes you think that I'm a virgin?

She shrugs. I don't know. There's something about you. Something vaguely...effete.

What's that mean, effete?

I'm not sure, she laughs.

Well I'm not a virgin.

Are you good in bed?

I've never had any complaints.

But are you any good?

Yeah, he says. I'm good.

She's got him on the defensive now, she's got the upper hand.

You wanna know how good I am?

She sits back and considers him. I'm not sure, she says.

He shrugs and looks away.

She waits him out.

He looks back at her. You're a very strange girl, he says.

No, she laughs. I'm not strange. I'm just a theater slut.

He looks at her, full of wonder. You certainly talk like one.

She is hurt by this, for some reason. She was feeling sort of proud of herself, that she dared to be this way. She found it oddly thrilling. She didn't know where it was coming from, but there is something about this guy, something about his lanky sinew, something about his arrogance, that makes her want to break him down. But now he gets superior—*you certainly talk like one*—and she feels smaller than before.

Well, she says. Maybe I'm all talk.

He studies her a minute. Are you all talk? he says. It is an innocent question, straightforward. He has stepped outside the box of this game, he has dropped his persona, and now he's just a guy asking her a question.

She looks at him, grateful the game is over. Yeah, she says. Pretty much.

He studies her a long moment. I don't think so, he says. He says it very evenly, aiming the words like a laser beam, and it sends a charge through her. She doesn't know how to react. She looks away. Then she looks back. He's still watching her, intently.

Maybe I ought to go, she says.

He watches her. She doesn't move.

Let me show you my sculpture, he says.

11

Well then, says Gillian. Let's have a look.

Harry steps into his painting corner and turns on the lights he works by, then steps back as if he were making room in a crowded elevator as Gillian slides into the space beside him, then turns to look at the painting.

Oh Harry, she breathes at first glance. That's lovely. She looks at him and back at the canvas. What is the problem? I think this is *lovely*.

Harry balls up his face. It's not right.

I love the composition, she says. The way the piano top slices the frame. It completely reorganizes the space. It doesn't even read as a square anymore.

She moves in closer to the canvas. And I *love* the light from this little lamp, the way it falls on her shoulder. She traces the shoulder with her finger. That is really quite lovely. She steps back to consider it. Yes, I like that very much. She turns to him and smiles, then turns back to the canvas, taking it all in again. The colors are absolutely delicious. That green...

Harry registers her comments almost perfunctorily, like a greedy child receiving presents and setting each one aside at once, in anticipation of the next. He is pleased with her reactions, pleased to hear her pick out the details that he especially likes himself, but he keeps waiting for a 'but'. And soon enough, it comes.

I suppose it is a bit somber, she says. Is that what you intend?

She goes for the darker hues, says Harry.

The client.

He nods.

Has she seen it?

I sent her a JPEG last week. But she's never seen it in person. Do you really think it's somber?

Well, it's...subdued. Don't you think?

Oh Christ, Harry mutters. Now I've got something *else* to worry about.

I don't think it's a *problem,* says Gillian. It's just an observation.

Harry groans.

Gillian turns to him. What is it that's bothering you, my dear? You sounded so desperate when you called.

I don't know. It's Michael.

What, exactly?

I don't know. At first I thought it was his hand. I thought maybe he shouldn't be touching her. Maybe his hand should hover, the way he's sort of hovering, see? Like an angel in a Renaissance painting. So I spent two days painting out the hand then putting in a new one, and it isn't any better. In fact, I'm afraid I made it worse.

I think this hand is fine.

You do? Well then, what *is* the problem? It's driving me fucking crazy. He parks himself on his stool, rips open a pack of gum and stuffs a stick into his mouth without offering any to Gillian. I mean, I think they're good likenesses, he says, tunneling back to the painting. I think I really have captured Lindsay. That vulnerability and strength...

Yes, says Gillian. Yes, that's very good. It feels very... *resilient.*

Yeah. And then Michael leaning over her that way, as if he's about to speak, or as if he wants her to turn to him. That's just the way I'd envisioned it. But for some reason.... He throws up his hands. I mean, I figure it's gotta be fixable. I've had problem paintings before. Every painting is a problem, that's the whole idea. But you just move through it, right?

Right.

Like you're working an algebra problem, or something.

Right. And eventually you solve it.

That's what I keep telling myself. But it doesn't seem to be working.

I don't get it, says Gillian, turning back to the canvas again.

It's the *feeling* I'm getting from him, says Harry. I don't like the feeling I'm getting from him.

And that is...? What, exactly?

He feels...uncomfortable. He makes *me* uncomfortable.

She considers him a moment. This is the boy who killed himself, right?

Right.

She cocks her head and lowers her shoulders. Well no wonder he makes you uncomfortable.

Harry eyes her a moment, then sighs. I guess. He slumps on the stool and stares at the painting, his brow knotted up in confused concentration. Then suddenly he jumps to his feet and advances on the canvas, sticking his face into Michael's face. *What's the matter with you?* he says. *Your mother wants a picture of you. You can't do her that little favor?*

Gillian watches him, cautiously.

Maybe? she says at last. Maybe you ought to take a break. Work on something else for a while. Do some sketches, some explorations. Some doodlings for another painting, to work on when this one is done.

This has got to be done by Christmas, says Harry, checking his watch. That would be...eight weeks? I don't have time to fool around.

Gillian watches him. Harry darling, she says. I think it's making you a little dotty, holing up in here all day every day with a suicide victim. You need to get out among the living. Have you made a date with that waiter?

Harry rolls his eyes. I've got work to do.

She gives him a wise smirk. You've got work to do in that arena too.

12

When David has finished the Sunday paper, he folds it on the floor beside him and suggests he and Marjorie go for a drive. He doesn't tell her where they're going, doesn't tell her that they've got any destination at all, just lets her believe it's an aimless Sunday amble like they used to do all the time before the kids.

Marjorie seems to be charmed by the notion, perks up in a girlish way. A better reaction than he'd even hoped for. She goes upstairs to change her clothes and comes back down a little decked out—nice tweed pants, a cashmere sweater, a butter-soft suede jacket. It makes him proud when she gets herself up like this, she is clearly such a class act.

He puts on some decent tweed of his own over a turtleneck and angles his sporting cap, then backs the MG out of the garage, lowers the roof and pulls on his gloves. Marjorie ties a silk scarf over her hair and cinches it around her neck like the 50s movie stars used to do, then slips on her big black sunglasses. And the two of them set off into the sparkling wind-swept day.

For the moment, it feels as if some of their old magic has come back. The glamorous young couple out for a Sunday spin in their roadster, cutting a swath through the countryside trailing laughter and high spirits. *Who was that couple?* he imagined people saying as they disappeared around a curve or over the crest of a hill. They were bright and they were beautiful, successful in every way, always had been and always would be. Forever the class president and the homecoming queen, a team.

They drive into the country, stop at a stand to buy some apples—Marjorie thinks that maybe she'll bake a pie, she hasn't baked in ages—then David checks his Rolex and pulls out a map.

What are you looking for? says Marjorie.

Just trying to figure out where we are, he says. There's something I want to check out.

What's that?

Something I saw in the paper. You'll see.

About one, they pull up in front of the farm. It is a handsome old thing, big hickories towering over it, fields stretching off all around it. There is a barn and a few lesser buildings and there is the house itself, imposing on its gentle rise. White pillars, green shutters, classic. David pulls into the drive and comes to a stop at the portico.

What is this? says Marjorie, half excited, half alarmed.

Just a little something I saw in the paper. Live the Life of a Gentleman Farmer. It's an open house.

It's for sale?

It's for sale.

Marjorie watches him get out of the car and stand there, assessing the place. Nice grounds, he says, looking around. Looks to be in pretty good shape. He glances at her. You like to look at houses, he says. Come on. Imagine what you would do with this one. He can feel her hesitating so he just moves on, leading the way, confident that she will follow.

In the entrance hall, the broker is waiting to welcome them in, decked out in tweed of her own. The hall is tall and ample, gleaming wood floors and pocket doors, a grandfather clock clicking off the seconds. She shows them into the dining room and asks them to sign in, then gives them the information sheets and invites them to look around. David can't imagine they're going to get all that much traffic out here in the country, especially with this asking price, but that's none of his concern. They move into the kitchen—it's old, it would need updating—then across the hall to the study.

This would make a nice office for you, he says.

For me? she says. David?

What?

What are you talking about?

Well don't you think this is kind of neat?

It's beautiful. But—

Look at the view you'd have from your desk, here. We could have packs of dogs.

What are you talking about?

Come on, he says. Let's just imagine it.

He heads back into the hall and up to the front parlor—a handsome old fireplace with built-in bookcases on either side, a cozy gathering of sofas around—then he climbs the stairs. The stairs are wide and highly polished, three different kinds of baluster in an alternating rhythm. He trails his hand along them as if he is stroking a harp, to draw Marjorie's attention to them. On the landing there is a reading nook overlooking the back forty, and then three bedrooms on the second floor with a single bathroom, in need of renovation. Marjorie has drifted off, caught up with some detail to her liking—he hopes—but she catches up with him on the sleeping porch off the back.

Look at this! he says when she joins him. A sleeping porch! I've always wanted a sleeping porch!

Marjorie leans against the doorjamb. What's gotten into you? she says.

Just looking, he says.

You actually thinking you want to move?

Well, he says. You never know. We've been where we are for some time. And now that the kids, now that Lindsay's gone.... He turns toward her, shoves his hands in his pockets and leans against the windowsill. Maybe it's time to move on, he says simply. He watches for her reaction.

It is she who looks away first. Here? she says. Way out in the country?

He shrugs. Not necessarily. But it might be nice, don't you think? The Life of a Gentleman Farmer? We could have some animals. Plant some crops.

Plant *crops?*

Well, a tomato plant or two, at least. I don't know. It could be fun to live out in the country, don't you think?

Lonely, she says. What about all our friends?

They could come visit. It's not that far.

He watches her cross to the windows, look out. She isn't taking to this idea, this is going to take some work. But that's OK. They can work on it together.

She fingers the mullion absently. Don't you think, she murmurs, that we've had enough upheaval?

He watches her. This is the moment. This is the very crux of it.

I feel like it's time to move on, he says. Maybe not here, but somewhere. That house.... He stops, unsure of how to continue. Doesn't it feel claustrophobic to you? With Michael's room up there? With that woods...?

And here he gets the momentary flash, the sudden surge of memory that bolts through his mind at times without warning, like a flash of lightning in the night, illuminating the darkness. Michael, in that woods. On that rock, his head splattered open like a smashed pumpkin. A punch in the gut that sends you staggering backward, all the wind knocked out of you. The image is there, then gone, shut out, until it breaks in again next time.

David lurches to his feet, heads for the door. He has to get away from this, to move into another room where maybe the image can't find him, at least for a little while.

David? says Marjorie.

He turns to her. I feel like I've got to *move,* he says. I've got to get *out* of there. *We've* got to get out of there.

I don't think you remember how much trouble moving is.

I don't care!

And we've got all the trouble we need right now.

Marjorie? He pleads with her. There are tears in his eyes. I can't...

She just stands there and looks at him, unable to do more than stare.

Can't you just think about it? he says.

She takes a deep breath, lets it out.

I guess, she says. I can think about it.

And that feels like a triumph. A tiny step, a triumph. He takes a tiny step toward her. That's all I ask. Just think about it.

She looks at him, searching his eyes. Then she lets her gaze drift to the door, slides her sunglasses back on and heads down to the car.

13

Lindsay is lying in bed. Aldo is in the bathroom.

She hates it when he leaves the room, the sudden cold that comes over her, as if he'd actually sucked the heat from her body and made away with it. She hugs his pillow as if it were him, trying to soak up the last remains of his body heat, his presence. She looks around the room—the clothes on the floor, the bottle of wine by the bed, the stacks of books and CDs, the posters. It has become a familiar landscape in the past few weeks, almost more familiar than her own room, but only in the way a foreign country becomes familiar—she is always aware that she is here on a temporary visa and could be deported at any moment.

Still, there is something enticing about being left alone in this room without him. The mystery of him, now, all around her, and she free to roam at will. She slides out of the bed and puts on his shirt, then pads across to his desk, her heart beating a little too hard. She looks at the photos pinned to the wall above it—some whack-o tilt-a-whirl architecture, some temples, some ruins, some rock formations—and scattered among them some pictures of people. One of them shows five people sitting around a picnic table, a couple of dogs nearby. One of the people is Aldo, probably last summer. Two adults appear to be his parents—or, rather, his mother and her new boyfriend; Lindsay has learned that much about him—and there are two kids, who must be his brother and sister.

She untacks the photo from the wall and holds it for closer inspection. She's never had a good look at it, for all the time she's spent here. The sister seems to be Aldo's age, maybe a year or so older; the brother is younger, and looks like him. They are seated next to each other. Aldo has his arm draped loosely over his brother's shoulders and he is smiling, he seems quite content. It's not a smile she recognizes in him. It's different from the smile he gives her—warmer, more relaxed. Why doesn't he smile at her that way?

She pins the photo back to the wall and gazes at the stuff on his desk, then picks up a sketchbook and flips through it. They are pencil sketches—who knows what they mean? Shorthand notes to himself in a language only he understands. But she likes the energy in the lines, the impulsiveness of the gestures. Sort of like Aldo himself.

She's only known him a few weeks now, but she has been with him every moment, or at least every moment he's allowed it, and it is almost exhausting being alert to him all the time, tuned to his every nuance. And when she's not with him, she's thinking about where he is, what he's doing, when she'll see him again. She has never fallen for anyone like this and she can't quite figure out what it is about Aldo that's so compelling.

He's not the kind of guy she'd ordinarily be attracted to. Or at least not the kind of guy she'd expect to fall head over heels in love with, if that is in fact what she's done. He's moody and self-absorbed, and at some level it seems he doesn't quite take her seriously. But she can feel it in her throat, all the time. The excitement of him, the hunger and fear. Her body aches at the merest thought of him. The insides of her elbows ache, her rib cage aches, her throat. It's yearning. There's no other word.

She flips the pages of the sketchbook and a letter falls out. Addressed to Aldo in a feminine hand, postmarked in

New Jersey. She glances at the door, then back at the envelope. The return address is Hackensack. There is no name, just the address. She lifts the flap carefully and sniffs. It is not perfumed. But she can see it's handwritten. Who writes handwritten letters these days? Doesn't this woman have email? It must be his mother, she thinks. Or his sister. No, his sister would have email. So it must be his mother. Or else some girlfriend, who thinks handwritten notes are romantic. He's kept the letter in his sketchbook; would he keep a letter from his mother like that? It's a letter he likes to read again and again; he carries it around with him. She glances at the door again. Then, with her heart pounding, she slips the letter from its envelope and unfolds it.

Dear Aldo,
I'm sitting in chemistry listening to a really boring lecture about nucleic acids and I thought of you. Of course. Nucleic acids always...

What are you doing? says Aldo.

She jumps and drops the letter.

What are you doing? he says, coming toward her.

I was just...she says. I was looking around.

He grabs the letter off the floor. You were reading my mail? he says, incredulous.

I was just flipping through your sketchbook...

You were reading my fucking mail?

It fell out of the book...

And you're wearing my shirt? What do you think you're doing?

I'm sorry. Really. I didn't mean...I wanted to see what you were working on, and the letter just fell out. I didn't mean...

Take off that shirt.

Aldo.

Take it off. He is furious now.

She unbuttons the shirt and he snatches it from her. Now she is standing there naked before him. He is wearing jeans and a T-shirt, bare feet, and she is naked before him.

He throws the shirt in the corner behind him without watching where it lands. What are you doing reading my mail?

He puts the letter back in the envelope, stuffs it back into the sketchbook. What makes you think you have the right to go through my stuff? he says.

I didn't think I had a right. I just...

Jesus Christ, he mutters. He stalks across the room, plants one hand on each side of the window and leans against it looking out, as if he is trying to push the wall over.

Aldo, she says. I'm sorry. I'll never do it again.

That is for sure, he says.

She goes to him, snakes up behind him, puts her arms around his chest. I'm sorry, baby. I'll never do it again. Will you forgive me, please? She likes the feel of her nakedness against the roughness of his clothes. She kisses his neck, fondles his chest. Please?

You know? he says. He turns to her. I don't think this is working so hot.

What?

This...thing. This relationship. I feel like you want too much of me. You want to be with me all the time. I can barely go to the bathroom alone. Then when I do, you go through my stuff...

Aldo, I'm sorry about the letter. I don't know what came over me. It was just there and...She sighs. I just want to know everything about you. I want to explore every corner of you.

He fixes her with a hard gaze. Did it ever occur to you, he says, maybe I don't want that?

She puts her arms around his neck, then runs them down his back to his butt. I want to possess you, she says, all throaty, trying to turn things sexy again, to get him off this awful topic.

Well, I don't want to be possessed. He pushes past her to the bed, sits down and lights a cigarette. Put on your clothes, he says.

She plops down on the bed beside him, tries to snuggle up to him. Don't you want to come back to bed? Don't you wanna play Hide the Salami some more?

He snorts. In amusement? she wonders. Or disgust?

Aldo, she coos. I'm sorry. Really. I didn't mean anything by it. I just sort of looked at the letter. I wasn't going to read it. She has her hand under his T-shirt now, she is kissing his neck. I'll never do it again, I promise. I'll never go in your stuff again.

He seems to be softening toward her, he's gone all silent and brooding now, the way he sometimes gets before they make love. If she can just get him past his anger, then she can manipulate him back to where they were before, warm and sleepy, making love in a lounging way. She knows he wants to come back there with her, so she just keeps working on his chest and his neck, and whispering into his ear.

Won't you forgive me, baby? she coos. Won't you forgive and forget? I'm sorry. I'll never do it again. I promise. I'll never do it again. She unbuttons his jeans. I'm sorry, she coos. She reaches down inside his pants and takes hold of him gently. Won't you forgive me, baby? she breathes.

Aldo mashes out his cigarette and exhales in one loud rush. Then he turns and pins her back on the bed. You wanna get fucked? he says. Lindsay is startled by this, and a little scared. He has her wrists clamped in his fists, he is kneeling over her, his face near hers. I'll fuck you silly, he says.

For a moment she is truly scared, not so much because she thinks he is really going to hurt her as because she feels, in that moment, that maybe she would like him to. At least she would have his full attention. She would have him, then, by the balls. Does he see that in her eyes? Something changes in his eyes and he rolls off her onto his back, groaning, staring at the ceiling. She lies beside him, listening to his breathing, wondering what just happened, what is going to happen next.

Suddenly he sits bolt upright. Put on your clothes, he says. He grabs some socks off the floor and starts to put them on, then grabs a shirt and pulls it over his head.

Where are you going? she says. She feels strangely like a child now—helpless, about to be punished. She wants to whimper, to suck her thumb, but she just pulls the sheets up to her throat and holds them there like a bouquet of flowers.

I'm going to work.

Can I come?

I'm going to *work.*

I won't bother you. I can sit in the corner and study.

Lindsay, put on your fucking clothes!

She starts to scramble for her jeans, her top. He stands over her, waiting, scowling at her. She feels like a dog, scolded by its master.

Hurry, he says.

I can't find my shoe.

Jesus Fucking Christ, he mutters.

Finally she finds the shoe and pulls it on and he goes to the door, stands there holding it open like a bouncer. Come on, he says. Let's go.

I need to brush my teeth.

You can brush your teeth at home.

Aldo…

Come on, he says. Move it.

They walk down the street toward his school without speaking. He is walking fast, and smoking; she has to hurry to keep up, pulling her jacket on.

When am I going to see you? she says. Want to meet for coffee later?

He doesn't answer right away. Did he even hear her? But when they stop at the light, he flicks his cigarette into the street then turns to her, exhaling. I don't think so, he says.

You want to study together tonight? We could—

I don't think so.

Aldo, she says. I'm sorry. Really. I didn't mean anything. She places a hand on his chest, a proprietary, calming gesture. He looks down at it as if he's discovered a bug is crawling on him and she puts her hand behind her back.

The light changes and he turns to go.

Give me a call, OK?

But he is running across the street now, eager to get away from her. She watches him duck into the studio entrance without turning to wave.

Or I'll call you, she says.

14

Harry has covered the painting. It stands on its easel now in the corner, draped with a sheet, like a ghost. Appropriate, Harry thinks, looking at it from his kitchen. Maybe he should paint the kid with a sheet over his head, like the ghost he is. But his attempt at whimsy doesn't amuse him.

The doorbell rings, and Harry starts. He's been waiting for the bell to ring, but it makes him jump anyway. His nerves are so jangled already from his constant frustration over that painting that he's become a stammering fool. And now this prospect at his door? He wants to crawl right out of his skin.

He forces his breath out three times fast, then buzzes the buzzer and climbs the stairs. He parks himself casually at his door and waits for the lift to arrive, trying to arrange himself so his nervousness doesn't show.

The lift arrives, the gate slides back, the door opens and there is Patrick, the waiter, in a T-shirt, jeans and a baseball jacket with the sleeves pushed up to reveal his forearms.

You found your way, says Harry.

Yeah, says Patrick, holding Harry's gaze as he approaches. He's got a confident swagger and a mischievous spark in his eyes but his eyes, as he comes closer, reveal all the warmth that Harry remembers.

Nice to see you, Harry murmurs, gesturing to the door. He follows Patrick onto the balcony and pulls the door shut behind them.

Nice place, says Patrick, looking around.

Harry would swear he can feel an electric current buzzing between their shoulders, but Patrick doesn't seem nervous at all. In fact he just seems calmly intent. Harry finds it very smooth. It makes him think there is nothing to fear.

Would you like some coffee? he says, leading Patrick down the stairs.

Got any beer?

I got beer, says Harry, relieved. He pulls two bottles out of the fridge—this will help to calm him down—and when he returns to the studio he finds Patrick has taken off his jacket. Sure enough, his body is well-toned, as promised.

So, says Patrick, looking at all the paintings on the walls. You gonna hang me up there? He turns to Harry and grins, hands on hips.

Harry's pulse flutters in his throat. We'll see, he says. You never know. He hands Patrick his beer and they stand there for a moment, making small talk about the paintings. But it doesn't have the same courtly feel it usually has with clients and subjects—in fact, it feels downright awkward, all of it obvious preamble. So finally Harry clears his throat. Why don't I sketch while we talk? he says. Just to see where it gets us.

Fine with me, says Patrick. He spreads his arms. Where do you want me?

Let's put you on the couch, says Harry. In that shaft of light there.

Patrick sits, as instructed, while Harry settles himself in an easy chair and pulls out his pad. He looks up and studies Patrick a moment. Can you lean forward a bit? he says. With your elbows on your knees? Yeah, like that. That's good.

So, he says, beginning to draw. Are you from around here?

Yeah, says Patrick. Lawrence. You?

Michigan, says Harry.

Never been there.

No reason to go. Although it's beautiful in the north.

He has Patrick fold his hands on a book and does some details of his hands, with those rings. Then he concentrates on the shoulder—the line of the neck, the shoulder, the arm. It is a beautiful line.

Harry sketches for maybe twenty minutes while their conversation ambles from topic to inessential topic—Mike's Gym, Boston, Ciao Bella, painting, and Patrick's simmering ambition to Do Something With Film—and when Patrick is ready for a second beer Harry switches to his camera.

It is interesting, he thinks, that he hasn't put on any music. Except for their conversation there is only the click of the camera, the sound of traffic rushing by, and Harry's quiet commands. Bend. Stretch. Look this way. Lower your chin. That's good. He likes the utter control he has, or imagines he has. The sparest instruction—*lean*—and the instruction is followed, no questions asked. When he asks him to take off his shirt, he does. When he asks him to take off his shoes, he does. Then he wants to ask him to take off his pants, but he doesn't quite dare.

But Patrick turns to him. Would you like me to...? He spreads his hands. He wears a little smile, a little quixotic, a little sly, like he's making an inside joke between them. But it isn't a challenging joke, as it might be. It's more like he's saying, simply, Do you want to take this step?

Harry lowers his camera and swallows. If you're comfortable...

Patrick turns away, as if he's being modest, and slips out of his jeans. He tosses them on the couch then turns to Harry, fully naked. Harry has to swallow hard to get the lump out of his throat. It's been so long since he's been so close... He takes a deep breath.

Yes, he says. That's nice.

He has Patrick do some poses with a kitchen chair— straddling it backwards; sitting sideways; one foot up, elbow on knee—and realizes that in all these poses he's keeping Patrick's back to him. He is only photographing his *back*, for Christ's sakes. He shakes his head at his sorry self, then asks Patrick to turn around and straddle the arm of the easy chair. He takes a number of shots that way, then has him sit down in the chair. After a few more shots, he suggests they get some of Patrick lying down.

Let's go in the bedroom, he says.

He can't quite believe he's said it. But Patrick is so calm about it all, so uncomplicated—Sure, he says, whatever—that Harry thinks maybe it's OK. That's what's so attractive about him, Harry realizes as he steps aside to let him pass, then follows him toward the bedroom. He seems so *uncomplicated*. What you see is what you get. It's so different from the way that Harry's been feeling lately. With that miserable painting, with himself. This is such a relief, to be with someone so straightforward.

They move into the bedroom, and Harry shoots Patrick gnarled up in the sheets as if he were sleeping. Maybe this would make a good painting, he thinks. This morning-after feel. Maybe he'll do a lot of paintings of Patrick. But finally Patrick stretches and rolls on his back and lays a hand on his thigh. Aren't you tired of taking pictures? he says.

I'm almost done, says Harry.

Don't you want to rest?

Harry looks at him, there in his bed. Patrick spreads his legs a little and looks at Harry with intention. His gaze is so tight and intense you could perform a high wire act on it, which is exactly what Harry feels he is doing. He stares into Patrick's eyes. All he has to do is step forward. All he has to do is sit down. All he has to do is move.

Come on, says Patrick. Come here.

Harry lowers himself to the edge of the bed with the camera in his lap. Once again he tries to swallow down the lump in his throat.

Patrick rises up on his elbow and lays a hand on Harry's back. You seem nervous, he murmurs, rubbing gently.

Harry swallows again, and nods.

No need to be afraid of me.

I know, says Harry. I mean, I believe that.

Patrick slides his hand up to Harry's neck and pulls him closer. His touch is so warm, his lips are so soft, it sends shivers all through Harry's body. And he feels that lump in his throat getting bigger. He'd forgotten all about this—the knee-weakening sensation of skin on skin, the impossible warmth, the trembling full-body alarm. What god invented this? But when Patrick starts to pull Harry down, he suddenly jerks away.

What's the matter? says Patrick.

Harry sits up and shakes his head. It feels like he's going to burst into tears, or drown. Uh, he says. I can't do this.

Patrick looks up at him. Huh?

I don't...says Harry. He clears his throat. I thought I could do this. But I guess I can't.

Patrick sits up. What's the matter?

Harry shakes his head. I had a bad experience a few years back...

What? says Patrick. What happened?

Harry stands and sets the camera on the bureau. It's not something I like to talk about.

Patrick considers him a moment, then seems to reach some conclusion. He peels back the sheets, then gets out of bed and sidles up to him. Maybe it's time for a *good* experience, he murmurs, putting his arms around Harry. Harry backs away, toward the kitchen. I think you'd better get dressed, he says.

But I like you, grins Patrick. Don't you like me?

I'd like you better if you got dressed. Harry darts out to the studio, gathers Patrick's clothes and brings them back to him. Here, he says. Please.

Patrick takes the clothes and stares at him, puzzled, registering now that this is not a coy game that Harry is playing, he really does mean to stop things here.

I don't mean to offend you, says Harry, hunching his shoulders and looking away, shoving his fists deep into his pockets. It isn't you. It's me.

Patrick starts to pull on his pants. What's the matter? he says, more clinically now. You mangled or something? You don't function right?

Yeah, says Harry. Something like that.

Patrick pulls on his T-shirt and tucks it in. Hey man, he says, buttoning his fly. I'm not into performance. I'd just like to be with you. If something happens, that's great. And if it doesn't, don't worry about it. He buckles his belt. It'd just be nice to be close for a while. He moves closer to Harry. You know what I mean?

Harry can feel the heat from Patrick's body, can feel the helplessness rise in his own throat.

You know what I mean? says Patrick more softly, moving in still closer. He slides Harry's shirt back off his shoulders and lets it drop to the floor, then presses himself up close, pushing

Harry against the wall. Harry turns his face away but Patrick presses in still tighter. You said you like my arms, he whispers, nibbling on Harry's earlobe. Well, I like your arms too. He slides his hands up to Harry's shoulders then runs them down the length of his arms. He lifts Harry's palms to kiss them, and to kiss his arms, but then he stops himself.

Hey, he says. What's this?

Harry looks down at Patrick, looking down at his arms. He closes his eyes. War wounds, he says. Then he slips away to the door. Look, he says. I'd rather you'd go.

Patrick stares at him, confused. Harry just watches him. Then Patrick pulls on his baseball jacket and follows Harry out to the stairs. Two steps up, he stops and looks around at all the paintings. He turns back to Harry, curious. Is this what you do? he says softly. Just pictures?

Harry doesn't answer.

I mean, is that your thing? Just pictures of guys? To jack off to, or something?

Still Harry doesn't answer.

Patrick studies him, puzzled. Then he gives a little shrug. Well, he says. Whatever. Good luck.

Harry watches him climb the stairs. On the balcony, he turns. See ya, Sport, he says. And then he is out the door.

Harry slumps on the arm of the couch, staring after him. Then staring at all his pictures. Then finally staring at the floor. He picks up the empty beer bottles and puts them in the recycling bin, then drags himself back to the bedroom. He stops in the doorway and looks at the bed, thinking that only moments ago there was a living, breathing person asking Harry to join him there. A living presence. An actual person, radiating warmth. And now there are only tangled sheets. Harry's empty, empty bed.

He sits down on the bed again, imagining Patrick is still there. Imagining his warmth. He picks up the pillow and hugs it to him, and for a moment he wants to curl himself around it and cry, or die. But instead he jerks the pillowcase off and tosses the pillow on the chair. Then he yanks the sheets from around the mattress and stuffs them into his laundry bag. He's surprised with how much force he does it. But if he can't do anything else, he thinks, at least he can do the fucking laundry. He goes to the bathroom and grabs his towel, then grabs the dishtowels from the kitchen, and he's halfway up the stairs when he remembers the sheet hanging over the painting. He stomps back down the stairs and across the floor to the easel, then lifts the sheet from the canvas. And there it is, that miserable painting, in all its confounding wrongness. He stares at it and his shoulders slump. He pokes the sheet into his bag and slings the bag over his shoulder, then looks at the painting again.

Well Michael, he says at last. He sighs. It looks like we're stuck with each other.

15

Marjorie has just come upstairs, carrying David's shirts, when she notices the door to Michael's room is ajar, at the end of the hall.

That door has been shut since Thanksgiving. Firmly shut and, she thought, locked. She knows that in time she'll have to deal with that room and everything in it, but she also knows there is no way that she can deal with it yet. So in the meantime she lives beside this Don't-Dare-Go-There area like the Brambly Woods or the Murky Mire on some treasure map in a children's book. She has actually gotten to the point that she hurries when she is in this hallway. Every day she walks this hallway, several times a day, with her shoulders hunched and her eyes on the floor almost as if she were trying to keep the room from seeing *her*.

But here now, the door is open. Is it Luz, gone in to clean? It isn't her day to be here. It isn't David; David's at work. Is it a burglar?

Is it Michael?

She actually feels a lurch of hope. Irrational, inexplicable. There.

She walks down the hallway toward the door. It almost feels to her like the hallway is lengthening as she walks, the way it does sometimes in dreams, the doorway receding even as you approach. But then there she is, at the door. She listens. Nothing, no sound at all. She raises her hand as if to knock, then lowers it to the knob and pushes. The door swings open soundlessly.

It is so quiet inside, so impossibly still. She stands at the door for a very long moment, afraid to disturb the stillness, afraid if she disturbs it the entire room might crumble to dust, like something so ancient it falls apart when touched. She reduces her breathing to almost nothing, then finally takes a tentative step. The room seems to hold together all right; her presence doesn't destroy it. She takes another step, then another. But she keeps herself small and quiet, the way she used to keep herself in church, in the presence of all that mystery and power.

She collects herself and looks around. It's all just as she remembered it. The varsity letters on his wall, the Dartmouth pennant over his desk. The posters—Nirvana, Soundgarden, Pearl Jam. Kurt Gibson, Barry Sanders. Footballs, baseballs, caps and gloves. All his stuff, all just waiting for him. Just waiting for him to walk in, home from school. Waiting for him to drop his pack on the floor and throw himself across the bed to make a telephone call. Waiting for him to feed his fish, then bounce a whiffle ball off the wall and dunk it in the wastebasket. To dump his clothes on the floor and wander off to the shower. It's all just waiting for him, as if he might walk in any minute. Cheerful, casual, hungry. Michael, her son, home from school.

Cradling David's shirts in one arm, the way she used to carry schoolbooks, she crosses the room to Michael's bed and slowly lowers herself, testing first with her free hand to be sure the bed will support her. Then she composes herself anew. Here it is, his little world. Michael's World, still intact. She's always loved this room. She devotes a big part of her life making rooms beautiful. She's studied it, perfected it. She's spent fortunes of clients' money on it, and she is good at it. But this, she thinks, is the most beautiful room she has ever seen. Like a field of rampant wildflowers no florist could ever outshine.

She looks about the room with wonder, and then it comes over her. Michael, sick in bed, surrounded with coloring books and toy soldiers. His smell of sour milk, his bib with the duck. Michael, playing ball in the driveway. Teasing her at her birthday party. Michael, in his wrestling togs. Coming in late, slightly drunk. Michael, taking the car alone and being gone for hours at a time. There are so many people in this room, it is overwhelming. And where is the one among them who would murder all the rest? Where is the culprit in the crowd?

Was it during that time in junior high, when he withdrew for a year or so, private and preoccupied? Was that more than just adolescence? But then he came back with such force, such brightness, like a comet returning out of the darkness, trailing a blaze of light brighter even than before. He lit up the room by just walking in. Michael, the magical presence. His friends, his smiles, his laughter.

Michael.

She looks up at the bulletin board covered with clippings and photographs, programs and dried-out boutonnières, letters and party invitations, and at the banner stretched above it: SECOND PLACE IS THE FIRST LOSER. She remembers the day he made that banner, the day his high school team lost an important wrestling match. He was so upset about it he shut himself in his room and didn't come out until the next day. They all pussyfooted around the house, wondering what to do. Lindsay tried to talk to him, but he told her to go away. Marjorie tried to take him food but he wouldn't eat anything. Only David honored his silence. Only David seemed to understand.

Just let him be, he said. And he said it with his eyes on the ceiling, as if he could see through the floor of Michael's room, could see him up there working something out. And his expression was determined, focused, as if he were beaming something up to his son. Some meaning, or understanding, particular to men and boys. As if Michael were going through some rite of passage that only a man could understand, that women and girls were excluded from.

Just let him be, he said. And not knowing what else to do, she did.

But the next time she went in his room, after things got back to normal, she found this hand-lettered banner on his wall, ferocious in its execution. This was what he'd been doing all that day. Measuring the letters, plotting them out, coloring them in with a studied obsessiveness. Going over and over them again, making them darker and darker, indelible. It broke her heart to see that banner, there was so much frustration in the pressure of the markers on the paper.

Marjorie feels her heart weaken. She can suddenly feel the weight of her blouse on her shoulders. The edge of the box in her lap. The constraint of her shoes, the rings on her finger, the bracelet on her wrist. All these forces pushing in from outside. And inside? Only yearning. Yearning to hold him, to soothe him, to comfort him. Yearning to touch him again, to smell his smell. To run her fingers through his hair, to feel him brush her hand away, laughing. To harbor him, to cure him. To save him.

And then a presence appears at the door, as if in her yearning she's conjured him, as if he's come back to this room after all. She looks up with a start and sees David. He is wearing a plaid shirt and chinos, carrying a briefcase.

Honey? he says. What are you doing?

She stares at him, unable to speak. She feels caught out naked, raw. Invaded.

He sets down his briefcase and starts to come toward her. Are you all right? he says.

She shrinks from him.

He pauses, perplexed. Are you OK?

Just leave me alone, she says.

Honey? he says. What's the matter?

Please. Just leave me alone.

But he won't leave her alone. He won't just let her be. He won't just let her work it out herself, the way he let Michael work it out himself. No, he has to interfere with her. He has to invade. He has to *push.*

He starts coming at her again. What's the matter? he says and she jumps to her feet, the shirt box falling to the floor. *Stop it!* she cries.

David gapes at her. What?

Stop *pushing!*

But Honey....

You always *push* too hard! You always pushed him too *hard!* She looks at her husband, blazing, hysterical. You always demanded too much of him! You were always in his face, *You've got to do better! You've got to do better!* She shakes her fists beside her ears. You wouldn't ever just let him be!

David goes suddenly pale. I...? he says. I...?

You! she sputters. You.... Then she runs from the room and David is left there looking after her as if every bone in his body has been crushed.

16

Lindsay presses the End Call button and stares up at the wall.

Once again, Aldo has not answered. Yet again, he has not returned her calls. She's been trying to reach him for days—is it weeks?—but he has shut her out completely, as if she never even existed. There was no discussion about it, no attempt to work things out between them. He didn't even give her the chance to air her views on the subject. He just made a unilateral decision, as if his actions didn't have an effect on anyone else at all.

She calls the number again, then again, hanging up when she hears the switch in the ring from his phone to his voice mail. There's no point in leaving another message. She's said whatever she has to say in her previous messages, and in the letter she sent.

She knows he's received the letter by now, the wrenching apologies, the promises never to violate his privacy again. She knows he's received the letter but she doesn't know if he's read it. He might have simply thrown it out unopened, or cut it up, or burned it. While he carries that other letter around in his sketchbook, reading it over and over.

She pushes the redial button again and chews on her lip while she listens. Her lip is almost raw by now but she can't stop chewing on it. She has to hear his voice again, even if it's only to let him tell her to fuck off. But after five rings, she hears the circuit switch over to voice mail again. She punches the End Call button three times, as if she were trying to strangle the phone, then she turns and hurls it onto her bed with all the fury that is in her. *You fucker!* she cries. *You miserable fuck!*

She stands there a moment, at a loss, then suddenly bursts into tears. She throws her window open and sticks her head out, screaming. *Aldo Ramirez is a fuckhole!*

A guy riding by on a bike looks up at her and flips her the finger.

Fuck you too, you asshole! she screams. *You stupid! Fucking! FUCK!*

She slams the window shut and turns back to her room, slumping against the wall. Why is the whole fucking world against her?

Her gaze comes to rest on a picture tacked to her wall, a reprint of a painting she picked up at the museum, a rosy-cheeked little girl in a bonnet standing in front of a doorway. She loved it for its delicacy, the subtlety of its coloring, the sweetness and trust of the little girl, her willingness and compliance. She pulls the poster from the wall, letting the push-pin fall where it will, and gazes at it a moment. Such a beautiful little thing. Then in a convulsion of disgust she tears it in half, and tears it in half again, muttering beneath her breath.

She strews the pieces on the floor and collapses on her bed. But the phone, hidden in the sheets, stabs her in the ribs. She fishes it from beneath her and hurls it hard across the room where it skims the top of her dresser and knocks a bottle to the floor, spraying glass and perfume in all directions.

Infuriated, Lindsay throws her pillow at the dresser too and all her bottles crash to the floor. She grabs the sheets and rips at them, the mattress bucking beneath her, then stands and pulls them off the bed and throws them on the floor. She grabs her shoes and throws them at the wall. She empties the wastebasket on the floor and throws it against the door. Then she stands there a moment, panting, like a bull in the ring between charges. With one last cry, she plunges at her bookcase, pawing all the books off the shelves, then pulls the whole thing over.

Then she stops, panting again, and looks around at what she's done. The room looks the way she feels inside, absolutely trashed, and there is something satisfying in that. She collapses at her desk into ball of self-disgust, holding her head in her hands. But even if tears would come, she knows that crying doesn't help. She's cried so much now it doesn't help anymore.

Exhausted, she sits back and looks at her desktop. The lamp has tipped over onto the script she's supposed to be working on. She sets the lamp upright then picks up the script and stares at it dully.

And you still don't know. Tony is one of them!

She tosses the script back onto the desk and stares at the wall a moment. Then, for lack of anything else to do, she opens the lap drawer and looks inside at the pencils and pens, the stapler, the paper clips, the ruler, the exacto knife.

And at that, her consciousness shifts into focus. Her whole being shifts into focus. She picks up the exacto knife and turns it around in her hand. A perfect silver cylinder, beautiful in its simplicity. She unscrews the cap, then sets it down carefully on the desktop, and fingers the cross-hatched grip, as subtly rough as a kitten's tongue. The way it catches the light gives it the sheen of something expensive and new.

She lays the flat of the blade on her finger, then rolls it from side to side, mesmerized by the way the light plays across its surface—a gleam, a glint, a sliver of silver, then black, then gray, then silver again. It leaves silver dust on her fingertip, glitter in the whorls of her prints.

She rubs the silver dust with her thumb, then presses the flat of the blade to her palm, watching the pillowed way it receives the pressure, the way the very tip of the blade catches the skin and then pulls free of it, making a little pinging sound, like a wind chime on a calm night.

She draws the flat of the blade across her palm as if she were honing it, listening to the faint twang it makes when it falls off the side. She sees it is leaving little white scratches there, rows of little white scratches like little white tattoos. She likes them. She likes the pattern.

She studies her hand. Such a mass of lines, such an intricate map. She traces the lines with the tip of the blade, pleased by the tickle and scratch, the sensual awakening.

So much going on in the palm of her hand.

So much going on.

She draws a new line on the heel of her palm, just a faint white scratch. Then she goes over it once, then again. Then she goes over it again, and again and again, every time pressing harder, feeling the tickle and scratch turn to sting when the blade finally punctures the skin and the blood begins to bead up. She winces at the sting of it, but the wince and the sting feel to the point, focused and incisive.

She is captivated now by the subtle seeping of scarlet— the bead, the bleeding line, as individual and expressive as an artist's brush stroke. Brilliantly colorful. She starts another line, next to it, studying the sensation of it, studying the effect. Then she draws another below it, and another, and another, tracing down toward her wrist. Watching with fascination the pliant resistance of the skin, its finally giving in, allowing the blade to enter. Watching the pattern revealed on her skin, the seeping scarlet grid.

She isn't thinking of Aldo now, she isn't even thinking of Michael. She's just focused on this tiny spot, this tiny part of the universe. It's like watching a nature show on TV, a study of tiny insects. Like dissecting something under a microscope. It is an experiment. A lancing of a wound, a bloodletting. And it does make her feel better. It makes her feel somehow centered again.

But then she hears someone unlocking the locks on her apartment door. Bobby is home, or Carol. She looks at her hand, a smear of blood, and her ears and neck go hot with shame. She grabs a T-shirt off the floor and holds it to her hand and her wrist, carrying the bundle before her as if it didn't belong to her, and darts across the hall to the bathroom, locking the door behind her.

17

Harry stands at his window, smoking, watching the rain drizzle down the pane. He wishes he'd gone to the gym this morning, even if only for long enough to get another massage.

He's been getting a lot of massages lately. He can actually feel the masseur raking the tension down the length of his arms and off his fingertips like static electricity, then shaking out his own hands as if he were shaking water off them, to rid himself of the tension he's pulled out of Harry's body.

They talked about it once, Harry and the masseur, that this is an occupational hazard for people in the massage business—they're always pulling tension out of people, then having to rid themselves of it so it doesn't accumulate. And Harry realized that's exactly how he feels about this painting—as if he is taking on the tension and pain of the people he's painting, and he has to find some way of keeping it all from accumulating in him.

He stabs his cigarette out in a saucer, exhaling in a great rush.

As if, he thinks. As if he could keep it from accumulating.

When the doorbell rings he buzzes the door, then climbs the stairs to wait. The lift arrives, the gate slides back, the door opens and out steps Lindsay, looking smaller than he'd remembered. She is wearing jeans, a black leather jacket and gym shoes; her hair is limp and wet.

Hello Harry, she sighs, as if she's just climbed the three flights of stairs.

Hi, he says. Thanks for coming.

She smiles a tired smile and turns into his studio, hiking her shoulder bag higher. He follows her down the stairs, a bit concerned at how worn she seems. Has she been taking care of herself? It's not a question he can ask straight out, so he just offers her a towel for her hair, and a cup of coffee, then joins her on the couch, lighting up a cigarette.

Harry? she says from under the towel. You're smoking?

Oh, he says absently, shaking out the match. Yeah.

They look at each other a moment, a moment of recognition, then Harry exhales a laugh. Want one?

She gives him a wry smile and holds out her hand with two fingers extended. He shakes a cigarette up from his pack and she pulls it out.

What happened to your hand? he says, lighting her cigarette.

She looks at the bandage, exhaling. Oh. Nothing, I burned myself.

Harry watches as she hunches over her coffee cup, mixing her witch's brew. There is something so fragile about her today. She is huddled inside her oversized jacket like an animal cowering in a cave, trying to hide from the elements, unsuccessfully. Pretty much how Harry feels himself.

You feeling OK? he says at last. You look a little peaked.

You sound like my mother, she says dully.

In absentia, he says. He watches her blow on the coffee, then take a tentative sip. You getting enough sleep?

She sets her cup down. No. She sucks at her cigarette and exhales in one long burst. I'm not sleeping much at all.

Partying too hard?

She gives him a tired smile. Now you *really* sound like my mother.

Oh, he says. Sorry. Don't you want to take off your jacket?

It seems to Harry the thought hadn't even occurred to her, as if she were too preoccupied to bother with such details. She pulls the jacket off and lets it slump on the couch behind her. She is wearing a flimsy little top, not really warm enough for Halloween weather, and it makes Harry want to wrap her in a blanket and bring her hot chocolate.

So, he says tentatively. What is it that's keeping you up?

She stares into her coffee. Oh just another failed love affair....

Oh? says Harry. Last time we talked, there wasn't any affair at all.

Yeah, she says wryly. Exactly.

Harry watches her. She seems to have a story to tell here, but he doesn't know if he's the one she'd want to tell it to. Still, he wants her to know he's available for it. What was his name? he says quietly.

Aldo, she says.

Harry waits, but she doesn't go on. Well, he says. I'm sorry to hear.

She nods, stirs her coffee. So what's up?

Well, says Harry, folding in on himself, crossing his arms and legs and curling up like a caterpillar that's been poked with a stick. I have some questions about this painting, so I wanted you to come have a look.

Lindsay exhales. What kind of problems?

Well, why don't we just have a look? he says. He stands and goes to the easel, a little dizzy from unfolding so fast. He turns it halfway toward her, then positions himself beside it so that as he completes the turn he will be facing her. It will give him a great view of her reaction.

She sits on the couch, elbows on knees. He steps back and completes the turn. In the first instant, she registers alarm. Is it just the surprise of seeing a picture, any picture, of herself and her brother? Then the alarm is replaced with a searching look. She cuts her eyes toward him, as if she is suddenly remembering he is there, then looks back at the canvas.

It's good, she says.

His heart sinks. That is not what he wants to hear. It's good: it's not so bad.

They're very good likenesses.

Harry watches her, withdrawing inside himself as if into a fortress.

She looks at him, then back at the canvas, then at Harry again. I don't know what else to say.

Do you like it?

Yeah, she says, unconvincingly.

You think your mom will like it?

Oh yeah, Lindsay perks. I think it's probably just what she has in mind.

Harry moves to the side of the canvas and turns to look at it, his elbow planted on his wrist, his fist held up to his mouth. Then he moves behind the couch, behind Lindsay, looking at it from her perspective.

Does Michael seem...right...to you? he says, fishing.

I don't know, she says. It looks like him, if that's what you mean.

Harry moves around beside her, looking down at her. How does he *feel* to you?

She looks up at Harry, then back at the painting. I don't know, she says. She seems to shrink inside her skin. It makes me feel cold, she whispers at last.

Cold? He *should* have given her a blanket. What do you mean exactly?

She crosses her arms, hugs herself. There's something...I don't know....

Something what?

There's something a little creepy about it, she says apologetically.

Creepy? says Harry, hollowing out. This is worse than he thought.

Not creepy, she hurries to say. But it's like.... It's like he's about to touch me.

And that feels creepy?

She looks at Harry, then back at the canvas. I don't know, she says, a little disturbed. It's just.... I don't know.

It's creepy, he says to himself.

It almost seems like he's going to grab me.

Grab you?

Yeah. She glances at Harry. It's like he's emerging out of the shadows there, like Jack the Ripper or something.

This is not at all what Harry had intended.

She laughs a nervous laugh. I'm sorry, this is just me. I don't know what I'm talking about.

No it's OK, he says. I want to hear.

But it's not the painting, it's me. This is just the way I've been *feeling* lately. Like he's following me, like he's right behind me.

And he's going to grab you?

I don't know.

He's going to hurt you?

I don't know. She considers Harry a moment, apparently wondering whether to go on, and something in his demeanor seems to convince her that he wants her to. She looks back at the canvas. Sometimes, she says tentatively. When I wake up in the night? I feel like he's there. In my room.

Michael?

It's not *him*, she says, glancing up. It's not like a ghost or anything. It's just this feeling, this kind of…presence. And it feels…just…*awful*. Like there's just no reason to go on.

Harry watches her a moment. He feels as if he's walked into a room and suddenly seen himself in a mirror he didn't know would be there. You've been experiencing that too? he says.

She looks at him with new interest.

He sits on the couch beside her, looking up at the painting. While I've been working on this thing, he says. I've been feeling that feeling myself, more and more. He lights himself a cigarette. It does feel like some kind of presence, he says. Some kind of…I don't know what to call it. He shakes out the match, exhaling. Maybe it *is* Michael, he muses.

Lindsay returns her gaze to the picture and a silence falls over them. Not because they've reached the end of what they have to say—it's clear to Harry it's not that kind of silence. It's more like they have arrived at a gate and both of them have paused, unsure of whether to go on. Harry doesn't know what the gateway is; it's clearly up to Lindsay to lead, if she decides she wants to. All he can do is wait. He can feel her rocking back and forth, her shoulder grazing against his.

Sometimes? she whispers at last. Since last year? She rocks back and forth a few times more. Especially in the last month. I've been scared I might do it myself.

Harry can feel her look at him, perhaps to gauge his reaction, but he stares ahead, still as a mouse. He doesn't want to disturb this.

She looks back at the painting again. It feels like Michael opened a door, she says, and now I can't ever shut it. I thought that door was locked and bolted. I thought that door was nailed shut. I didn't think it even *was* a door. But now that Michael's gone out through it, I can't think of anything else sometimes. It's like I'm in this room with this door and all I can think about is that door. It's like the door in an airplane or something, like the door skydivers jump out of. And there I am, all alone in the plane, and Michael has jumped out the door. And there it is, standing open. Blue sky, the wind rushing past. Just kind of begging me to jump. And I could do it, you know? I could just jump. I could just fly out the door, after Michael. It would only take an instant. Just the decision to go, then go. I could jump off of a bridge. Or in front of a car. Decision, go, done.

She stares at the painting, rocking. I guess that's what I mean, she says, when I say I feel like Michael's behind me, like he's going to grab me or something. Like maybe he'll push me out the door or something. I don't know, it's weird. She stops rocking and just stares at the canvas.

Funny, says Harry at last. Isn't it?

She cocks her head, curious.

He gazes at her a moment longer, then leans forward to knock an ash into the saucer. He doesn't really have to search for his resolve at this point, but he does take this moment to steady himself. A few years back, he sighs. He sits back and closes his eyes, takes a deep breath and lets it out, as if he's taking off too-tight clothes. About three years ago, he goes on, a friend of mine killed himself. He looks at Lindsay. Well, he murmurs, he was actually more than a friend. He was...

Oh, says Lindsay.

Yeah. And after that happened, I felt the same way. Like I wanted to jump ship too.

Why haven't you told me this?

Harry looks at her. This, he says, gesturing to the space between them, this is about you, not me. It wasn't my place to haul in my baggage.

But didn't you think I'd want to know?

He shrugs. Do you?

Yes. She turns on the couch to face him. What was his name?

Harry looks at her. Eric. He tilts his head toward the painting behind her. That's him there.

Lindsay turns to look. That's the painting you were working on the first day I came here, she says.

Oh yeah, says Harry, exhaling. Oh yeah. I've been working on that ever since he died and I still haven't got it right.

Huh, says Lindsay, studying the picture. A redhead.

Eric the Redhead.

What was he like? says Lindsay, turning back to him.

Harry sighs and smiles. Such a big question, Lindsay. He looks up at the ceiling, searching. He was funny. Intelligent. Sexy. He laughs. He was *very* intense. He looks at Lindsay, embarrassed. I'd always been the kind of guy who stood on the sidelines, watching. You know, I painted *pictures* of life. I was just an *observer.* But Eric pulled me into the game. He laughs, looks out the window. I'd never met anyone like him before. Every minute of every day with him was a full-out *experience.* The volume was turned up very loud. And I thought, wow. So *this* is what life is about.

How did he kill himself?

Jumped off the roof of his building. Twelve stories.

Why?

Harry closes his eyes. He was crazy. Kind of tortured. He used to burn his hands with cigarettes. I think it was that madness in him that was part of his drawing power, you know? Like maybe I could save him. He shakes his head. Or save myself. Anyway. I found myself having those kinds of feelings myself, afterwards. Like you said. You know. I was afraid I might do it myself.

Lindsay watches him a long moment, and when she speaks again her voice has changed. It is quieter now, more private, as if she is speaking to herself and allowing Harry to overhear. Sometimes I wish I *could* do it, she says. Sometimes I wish that *I* could go, too. It would be so nice to have it all done with. Nothing to worry about anymore. Nothing to feel anymore. Just floating in the big blue sky.

Harry looks at her. Then slowly he rolls up his sleeve and extends his wrist. She stares down at the scars on his arm, then looks up into his eyes. She rocks back and forth a couple of times with an odd, private smile on her face. Then silently she holds out her hand and peels the bandage back.

Harry looks at her scabs and his body jerks in a mirthless laugh. He looks up at her and it feels to him like all the doors have flown open all down the hall in both directions. And there they are, looking at each other.

Then Lindsay's eyes soften. Don't worry, she says, as if she is answering some question in his gaze. I'm not going to do anything. She tapes the bandage closed again. But I don't know what I *am* going to do. She looks up at Harry's painting. How do you get through this? she asks.

Harry studies her. Then he cocks a brow and sits back. I used to think working worked, he says, rolling his sleeves back down. If nothing else, it passed the time. He buttons his cuffs, reaches for his coffee, takes a sip and sets it down. Then he looks at the canvas across the room. But I'm not so sure anymore, he says. He looks at her, apologetic. I really don't know what works anymore.

PART III

18

David hesitates a moment to register what he's doing, then goes ahead and follows her in. It is an appealing apartment, snug and airy at once, definitely the apartment of a single woman in the city.

Nice, he says. Very nice.

Thanks, she says, dropping her jacket and bag on the couch. I like it.

How long have you been here?

About a year. Since the divorce was final. Would you like a drink?

He's a little surprised she asks this question so quickly. She might at least make a show of showing him the apartment first.

Sure, he says. A little scotch would be nice.

A little scotch it is, she says, moving into the kitchen.

You like living in the city? he calls after her.

Yes, she calls. I like it a lot. It's certainly a lot better than staying out there in the suburbs with all those boring married people.

She reappears with two tumblers. Sorry, she says. I know you're still married. She hands him his drink, then turns to survey the apartment. I was nervous about it at first, she says. I thought I'd be impossibly lonely. But in fact I'm liking it just fine. There are always people around. There are bookstores and cafés and shops. There's music at night, if you want it. I meet people. She turns back to him. It isn't a bed of roses but it isn't as bad as you think it will be.

David is heartened to hear this. He touches his glass to hers, holding her gaze as he does it. Well, he says. Here's to independence.

She cocks her head in approval, holding on to his gaze too, then abruptly turns to the window with its view of the building next door. I'd kind of hoped for a view of the river, she says. But the neighbors are sometimes intriguing when they don't know they're being watched. She turns to him and smiles. One of the kinkier advantages of living in the city. Want to have a look around?

Lead on, he says.

She shows him the living room with its fireplace, the kitchen with its little deck, the dining nook with its view of the neighbors, then she leads him up the stairs.

He is intrigued with the apartment—it's very downtown, very hip, very *young*—but of course he's far more intrigued with her. Very downtown, very hip, very shapely. Very available. He wonders if he's really going to do this, but of course he knows the answer already. *Because It Is Bitter and Because It Is My Heart.*

The guest room, she says. My office, she says. The bath. And this is the bedroom.

He stands next to her, looking in at her bedroom, the queen-size bed, the fabric draped above the headboard as if the bed were some kind of throne.

She turns to him. You like?

He looks at her smiling, and nods, heavy-lidded.

She smiles, pleased with the reaction.

Would you excuse me a minute? she says. I'd like to get out of these work clothes.

Sure, he says. He doesn't move.

She stands there looking at him, amused.

Haven't you heard? she says, stroking his tie. There are rules against fraternizing with the staff.

Are we fraternizing?

Not yet, she says, pushing him gently out the door and closing it part way.

He lingers at the door, leaning against the wall, amazed at how bold he's being with this. It's a role he hasn't played for a very long time but it comes back as easily as riding a bike, or swimming. It seems to be a muscle memory: how to hold yourself, how to pitch your voice. But of course it's more than just memory. Someone has to call it out. It doesn't just reappear on its own.

She reappears at the door in a loose-fitting jersey, no bra and bare feet. Oh, she says. Surprised to find him there, hanging at her door.

Comfortable?

She slides by him and heads for the stairs. I'm getting there.

Are we fraternizing yet? he says, following after her.

She stops and turns back to him, suddenly grim. We're not going to have an affair, she says with a scolding look. We can have a good time maybe once or twice. But I'm not getting myself involved with a married man.

Understood, he says, chastened, relieved. This is just a... dalliance.

Call it whatever you want, she mutters, turning away from him again.

It takes another drink and a half, but soon they are back in the bedroom again, not so much rolling around together as rolling over each other as if they were combat vehicles. Invading, pushing boundaries, relentless. It is not a kind of lovemaking that David is accustomed to—certainly not in recent years—and he is taken aback by it.

She climbs on top of him and slathers him with her tongue, working her way down to his crotch and going to work on him there, making him writhe and moan in a way he's not sure he's ever done before. He bucks and she fights him back down, her hands pressing firm on his hips. Then she pulls herself back up his torso, nibbling here, kissing there. When she reaches his nipple, she licks it and David is surprised at how sensitive it is. When she bites it, it shoots a dagger inside him, and he jerks in response, his dick growing stiffer.

Ohhhh, she says, rising up over him, her hair hanging in his face. You *like* pain.

He looks up at her, surprised to realize the answer is yes.

You *like* the pain? she prompts, jerking her knee against his balls.

He studies her twisted features hidden in the cave of her hair and feels something harden inside of him, spite.

I like the *apartment,* he says.

19

Lindsay returns to her position, plants her feet apart and bends straight-legged from the waist, stretching out her back. She twists her head from left to right, rubbing her neck to limber it up, then straightens and assumes her pose, one hand on her hip, the other above her knee as if she were holding the hem of her skirt. She lifts her chin and looks down her nose, haughty as a drag queen.

OK, calls Renee. Let's go!

The piano begins and everyone moves, swirling past each other, charging in teams, retreating, resuming, stamping their feet, clapping, hooting, a festival of high spirits, an angry, joyous competition. It is elaborate and difficult, confusing, but she does it better this time and when the piano reaches its final crescendo she is in the right place and her weight is correctly balanced so that Jerzy can lift her up onto his shoulder like a welter-weight champion. She tosses one arm into the air and tosses her head, triumphant. *Olé!* They hold the tableau for several counts and she feels her weight begin to sag. She can feel Jerzy struggling to hold her steady.

OK! cries Renee. We're getting there. Let's take a fifteen-minute break, then I want to do the Rumble. Sharks, Jets, fifteen minutes.

Jerzy sets Lindsay down and they fall against each other, laughing. I promise to cut out the doughnuts, she says.

He kisses her forehead. I'll add twenty reps on the barbell.

Lindsay? calls Renee. Can I see you a minute?

Lindsay grabs her water bottle and slings her towel around her neck, then joins Renee at the piano.

Honey, says Renee. What's the matter?

I don't know, says Lindsay, out of breath. I just...I don't know.

Well, I'm concerned about you. You're coming late to rehearsals. You don't have the steps, sometimes you don't even know your lines. What is going on?

Lindsay shrugs. I'm sorry. I just...I'm just tired, I guess.

Have you been to a doctor?

No. I'm not sick. I'm just tired.

Well you're really not keeping up. You're supposed to be leading the rest of the girls, you're supposed to be running this number, but you're sort of getting lost in the crowd.

I know. I'm sorry. I'll do better.

Renee shakes her head. You keep saying that, but I don't see it happening. She places a hand on Lindsay's shoulder, locks her elbow, stiff-arming her, and looks intently into her eyes. I know you can do this part, Honey. I know you've got it in you. But it almost seems like you don't want to. Do you really *want* this part?

Oh yeah, says Lindsay. Yeah, I do. This is a great opportunity.

But even as she says it, she can hear how hollow it sounds.

Renee nods at her, unconvinced. Linda is ready to step in, you know. She's got it all down pat already. If you don't get it together pretty quick, we may have to rethink this. OK?

Lindsay nods.

I'll give you a week, no more. I don't want you doing this if you can't do it like you mean it. She grabs her billfold from her bag, then looks at Lindsay again. Think about it, she says, then she heads for the door.

Lindsay watches Renee cross the room and pause to chat with Nicole, then she leans heavily against the piano, wiping the sweat from her neck. She stares at the scuffs on the dance floor, at the knocking radiators beyond, the piles of coats and books and bags, seeing none of it. All she can think is how badly she wants to be at home, alone in her bed.

When she finally gets back to her apartment, Lindsay finds that no one is there, that there isn't even a light on, no sign that anyone has been there, no sign that anyone lives there at all, and she feels her heart go still more hollow.

She lumbers into her room, exhausted, and falls across her bed in the dark, then rolls onto her back and stares up at the shadows the streetlights make on the ceiling. She listens again to what Renee said, playing it again in her mind, then listens to the fatigue in her bones, the emptiness in her lungs. She closes her eyes, concentrates on her breathing to try to center herself, but there doesn't seem to be any center. She feels like a human Los Angeles, a sprawling disorganized mess.

She rolls onto her side and stares at the dark shape of her pack beside her, then unzips the pouch and reaches in, pulling out her phone. She flips it open and stares at the glowing screen, a comforting little campfire, then punches in the speed dial.

She lifts the phone to her ear and listens to it ring, as if she is listening to a familiar song. Once. Twice. Three times. And then, amazingly, Aldo picks up.

Hello? he says.

She doesn't speak. She hears loud music in the background, the sound of someone laughing, a boy.

Hello? says Aldo again.

She opens her mouth to answer, but her lungs are so empty no air will come out.

Hel-*lo*? says Aldo, irritated.

Lindsay hears a sudden burst of loud talk. There is a party going on in his room. Aldo is having a party. She lowers the phone and looks at it, then snaps it shut and falls back on her pillow, looking up at the shadows again. She watches the way they move, mesmerized. Then, in the flickering darkness, a memory comes to her: sitting with Harry on his couch, peeling back her bandages as he rolls up his sleeves, the two of them almost laughing at the absurdity of it.

20

Harry has been sitting on his couch for what feels like hours, smoking cigarette after cigarette, his feet propped on the trunk. All he can see is what Lindsay saw, now—that sense of Michael not as an angel, not as a guiding spirit, but as a menace, a haunt, a danger. How could he not have seen it before? Michael, emerging from the dark; Lindsay, sitting there like prey. It's so obvious to him now, it makes him feel like an idiot.

But idiot or not, there it is, inescapably. And what can he do about it now? Change Michael's expression? Brighten the background? Try moving the hand again? None of those would do the trick, but what other options are there?

He moans and stretches out on the couch, gazing through the window at the dank November rain. Maybe he'll have to start over from scratch. Just slide this canvas under the stairs and stretch a new one. Return to the sketches, return to the photos, go back to Marjorie Davenport and tell her he has failed.

He lights another cigarette and exhales the smoke straight up. Then his gaze travels up to the painting of Eric on the wall above him, the painting he worked on all last summer, another towering failure. The most recent of the whole series of Eric paintings he's worked on since Eric died, all the rest of which he burned, because they were all such failures.

This one shows Eric in a doorway, the door partly open, his hand on the knob. Is he opening the door, to enter? Or pulling it closed, as he leaves? Every time Harry looks at it, it reads differently to him. And that is what's good about it: it captures Eric's elusiveness, his ultimate unknowableness. One day he would be there, all jabber and jokes and hijinks, dragging Harry out to some festival or flea market. But the next day he'd be gone, just gone, no one knew where. He'd just disappear, out of town, down a dark alley, who knew?

Harry could never tell how long he'd be gone. A day, a week, several weeks. Once it was over a month. And then he'd show up again, all smiles. Or sometimes, not all smiles. Sometimes he'd show up again with bloodshot, shell-shocked eyes, as if he'd just come back from a battlefield that was strewn with the dead and dying. Sometimes he'd have marks on him, as if he'd been thrashing through the jungle, or as if he'd been hurt, or hurt himself. There were the cigarette burns, sometimes, on his hands and legs.

It kept Harry constantly off-balance, never knowing if or when Eric would show up, never knowing what shape he'd be in. Always afraid, when he disappeared, that he wouldn't come back. A smarter person, a wiser person, wouldn't have gotten involved with him. A savvier person would have seen how dangerous Eric was—to himself, and to anyone who got close. But Eric had rescued Harry from his self-imposed exile: Harry, who had sentenced himself to solitary confinement with his brushes and pigments and rags. Eric was the one who shook him awake and brought him out into the world. Eric was the magician who held the keys to Harry's locks, and Harry was indebted for that. Even if it did mean he was still under lock and key.

Harry remembers coming home one night and finding a note on his pillow, written on a shirt cardboard. Eric had let himself into the studio and left this note, before one of his disappearances. The note explained that he had to go away for a while, that he didn't know when he'd be back, that he'd be thinking of Harry and dreaming of him, but for now he had to get away. Not from Harry, from himself. He was sorry. Harry shouldn't worry. He'd be back soon, and he'd bring ice cream.

Harry sat on the edge of the bed, overwhelmed. He knew he should have been angry at Eric for running off again. He should have been angry that Eric didn't talk to Harry face to face, didn't give him a chance to help in some way. He should have been downright bullshit, that's what Gillian told him he should feel. But what he felt was empathy. He understood what Eric was doing, and why he was doing it that way. He recognized it, inside of him. As if Eric's pain, whatever it was, had set his own to quivering. And in doing that, it had brought him alive in some way. It wasn't what anyone would have called a healthy relationship, Harry can say that now. But it was a relationship. No one had ever had a key to Harry's home before. And more than anything else, that night, Harry remembers feeling lucky that he could come home and find that someone had left a note on his pillow, with an apology and a promise.

But now here he is, alone again, staring up at this picture of Eric, still suspended in the exquisite torture of not knowing. And in this moment he knows he's had enough. It announces itself as a sudden fact. He has been stuck in this mire long enough. Eric escaped. Eric bailed out. And he isn't coming back, this time. But here Harry is, still waiting. And all the frustration he's been experiencing with the painting of Michael, on top of the frustration over all the paintings of Eric, on top of the frustration that Eric has finally gone off and will never come back...he just can't take it anymore. Something has to move, something *in him* has to move. If he can't solve the problem with Eric, at least he can deal with the problem of Michael.

He thrusts himself to his feet and crosses to his easel. He parks himself on his stool, squares the canvas in front of him, and stares at it, tight-lipped, his frustration hardening into a tightly focused intention. He knows what he has to do and he is coldly determined to do it.

He fumbles through the paints on his table and comes up with burnt umber. He squirts some onto his palette, then mixes it with black and turns to face the painting. He dabs a brush into the paint and takes a step toward the canvas.

Does he really dare do this?

What choice does he have?

He starts slowly, working with precision. He begins by drawing the shadows from behind Michael further forward, surrounding him in darkness. He obscures the back, then the shoulder, the arm. He brings the darkness over Michael's neck, his ears, the crown of his head, enveloping him as if in waves, until there is only the face left.

And then, with a deepening sadness, Harry dips his brush onto his palette and begins to paint over the face. The cheekbone first, so perfectly modeled. Then the eye, the nose. Slowly they go. The lips, the chin. A sickness knots in Harry's throat. Is he right to do this? He pauses with his brush in mid-air, stoking his resolve. *Something has to move.* So he sets the paintbrush to moving again, as procedural as a funeral cortège, slowly covering Michael over until he has disappeared completely and Lindsay is left there alone in the light.

21

All right, then! says Marjorie. It's settled! She pokes her notepad emphatically with her pen, to punctuate the plan. We'll arrive late on Wednesday night and go directly to the Ritz, you come over Thursday morning for a little breakfast before we go to Duxbury for turkey, then on Friday we'll go see the painting. OK?

Yeah, says Lindsay. That sounds fine.

You'll arrange the viewing with Mr. Garrett?

I'll call him as soon as we hang up. I'm sure it'll be OK.

Perfect! says Marjorie, placing her pen beside the edge of her notepad and adjusting it perfectly parallel. Absolutely perfect. She switches the phone to her other ear. I can't wait to see this painting!

I think you're going to like it, says Lindsay. I think it's just what you had in mind.

Marjorie nods as if she knew that. I had a good feeling about this guy.

He's scared to death you *won't* like it, though.

Oh, says Marjorie, waving a dismissive hand in the air. I know I'm going to love it. He's just got a case of opening night jitters, that's all. I'm sure it happens all the time.

You're probably right.

So tell me, she says in a warmer tone. Are *you* starting to get the jitters? How're rehearsals going?

Oh, sighs Lindsay. She skips a long beat, then another long beat. Not all that well, actually.

Marjorie sits up straighter, frowns. What do you mean? she says. What's the matter?

Well, Lindsay murmurs. The director's not all that happy with what I'm doing. She's actually talking about replacing me with the understudy.

Lindsay! says Marjorie, alarmed. She switches the phone back to her other ear. What is going on? What is this woman's problem?

Oh Mom, says Lindsay. I don't know. I'm just…She's right. I'm really not doing that well.

Well what is the problem? says Marjorie, leaning into the phone.

I don't know, Mom, Lindsay sighs. I'm just so *tired* lately.

Well are you getting enough sleep? Do you want me to get you some sleeping pills? I could call Dr. Greenberg…

No, it's not sleep, says Lindsay. I'm just tired of *everything*. You know what I mean? Don't you ever feel that way? Like you just don't want to put out the energy anymore?

Marjorie settles back in her chair, calculating her answer. Well sure, Honey. Of course. She picks up her pen and places the tip on the notepad, lets her fingers run down its length, then flips it end up and does it again. It has an oddly calming effect, a balancing effect. But you just keep putting one foot in front of the other, she says, and it passes.

Yeah, says Lindsay. I know.

Come on, says Marjorie softly. Buck up. You know you can do it.

I *can*. I just don't feel like I want to.

Lindsay, says Marjorie, annoyed. What kind of talk is that?

Defeatist Talk, Lindsay recites.

That's right. And we don't countenance that.

I know, Lindsay says, her voice small. Then, more quietly still: Mom? she says. Could I come home for a while?

Marjorie sits back, perplexed. Come home?

Could I just come home for a little while? A long weekend or something? I just feel like I want to sleep in my own bed. Maybe eat some of your waffles.

Marjorie sets down her pen askew. But what about rehearsals? she says. You can't miss rehearsals.

I could.

Now Lindsay, no. You're just tired right now. You just need a good night's sleep, that's all. I want you to go to bed early tonight and go back in there tomorrow and absolutely knock them off their feet. Just pick yourself up and do it. You know you can do it. You're a Davenport.

Yeah, says Lindsay. I know.

You'll feel better in the morning. You want me to call Dr. Greenberg?

No, I'll be OK.

I'll call you tomorrow, says Marjorie.

OK.

Don't forget to call Mr. Garrett.

I won't.

I'm looking forward to seeing you, Honey.

Yeah, says Lindsay. Me too.

When they say goodnight, Marjorie sets the phone precisely in its cradle then stares for a moment at her hand resting lightly on the receiver, composing herself. Then carefully she lifts her hand off and places it in her lap, feeling that for the moment at least she has kept things under control.

22

Lindsay pulls her coat tighter around her neck and leans against the wind off the river. This is more than autumn bluster today, more than the stormy swirl of winds that give fall all its drama and vibrancy. This is a full-out assault, a steady hammering of bone-chilling wind that stings the nose and dulls the mind and makes the blood start to thicken.

She waits for the light at Hemenway, huddling against the cold, wondering what the problem is. When she called Harry yesterday to arrange for her parents to see the painting, he sounded...well, what *was* that sound? Disturbed? Concerned? Scared? He wouldn't say anything on the phone; he just asked her to come over. No, that's not what he said. He said, *You'd better come have a look.* What did that mean? She just saw the painting last week.

The light changes and she scurries across the intersection, down the hill to the turnpike and around the curve to Harry's studio. It's so dismal today the turnpike traffic already has its lights on. She hurries up the stairs and shoulders inside, cursing at the cold.

When she steps off the lift, she finds Harry waiting not at the door of his studio, as usual, but at the door to the lift, as if he can't wait to see her. He looks absolutely terrible. Unshaven, unkempt, eyes glazed, smelling of beer and cigarettes. It's three o'clock in the afternoon but he doesn't appear to have washed yet today.

Harry, she says. Are you OK?

Yeah, he says. I'm OK. I'm just...sort of...wiped out. He lets out a helpless, self-mocking laugh and gestures loosely to his door, then follows her onto the balcony. She pauses at the railing to take the place in again—this entrance insists you stop to look around—and sees the canvas by the window, turned to face the studio. There she is, as she was last week, all pretty on the piano bench. But behind her now, Michael is missing. Where he stood before is just blackness, absence. For an instant, it almost feels to her as if he's died again.

She wheels to Harry. *What happened?*

He just gazes at her sadly. She turns back to the studio. And then she sees Michael everywhere else, in photos spread over every surface. As if he'd somehow escaped from the painting and scattered himself around the room. She looks back to Harry, speechless, searching for some clue, but all he does is look at her. She turns back to the studio, then slowly makes her way down the stairs, surveying the array of photos spread around the room. At the last stair she stops, listening to the pounding of her heart, then steps carefully onto the studio floor.

It feels a little like walking into a wake, but all the people at the wake are the same person. All of them, Michael. The person who died. It's fascinating, somehow, like being drawn down a dark hallway. She isn't sure if she's breathing. She moves among all the photographs. There he is in his black-and-brown checked shirt. There he is in Marina del Rey. There's his high school yearbook photo.

She looks up at the canvas again—just her by the piano, no Michael—then turns back to Harry as he arrives behind her on the studio floor. What happened? she breathes again.

Harry sighs. I painted him out.

Why?

He grabs an open beer off the coffee table. It was wrong, he shrugs.

But you've got to put him back in!

Well that was my intention, he says, taking a swig of his beer. But I've been staring at it and staring at it and nothing is coming to me. He turns to her and shrugs again. I'm afraid I've fucked it up for good. He fixes her with a bright, phony smile. And now your *parents* are coming to see it!

Oh Harry, Lindsay groans. I'm sorry. I didn't realize...

He waves away her apology. They've got to see it sometime.

But what are you going to do?

He collapses on the couch and lights a cigarette. I don't know. Maybe I'll try to renegotiate for a single portrait, or something. He exhales and looks at the canvas. The only problem is it doesn't work as a single portrait, either, it's so off-balance. He studies it a moment, eyes glazed. Although I suppose I could cut down the canvas, he muses. Make it a different size and shape...

Harry! cries Lindsay. This is crazy! I can't believe you did this! He looks up at her wearily and she realizes he doesn't have any interest in her amazement. She also realizes that he's a little drunk. She studies him, the mess he is in. Smoking, drinking, disheveled in the middle of the day. Photographs scattered everywhere. This is a guy, she thinks, who needs a friend. She clicks into a lower gear. Any more beer? she says.

He blinks at her in surprise. Yeah.

Can I have one?

I thought you had a class.

She shrugs off her coat and tosses it on a chair, cavalier. I've already got all the class I need. She steps into the kitchen and opens the refrigerator. There is almost no food inside, just some shriveled lemons and a few discs of old lunch meat, but there are two six-packs of Corona. She pulls one out and opens it, then goes back out to the studio and plops down on the couch beside Harry, staring at the painting. She is vaguely excited by it, she finds, as if he has done something naughty. She scrunches down into the cushions, licking the rim of her bottle, and they sit for some time in silence, the traffic rushing by outside.

I do like what I've got there of you, though, Harry says at last, more or less to himself. Without Michael there, it's even stronger.

What's stronger?

Your determination.

She studies the painting closer, trying to see what he sees.

I remember the moment I first saw it in you, he goes on. That day we were doing sketches and photos? The day you told me how Michael died.

Yeah.

I'll never forget that moment, the way you looked. It was just...hmm. It really touched me somehow.

Lindsay doesn't respond. He was touched by her? Really?

And then the next time we met, says Harry. That day at your school, remember? When you walked out in a huff?

Yeah.

There was something scary to me about that. I felt like whatever it was I'd seen in you—whatever little flicker of light—I felt like it was in danger of going out.

Lindsay tries to remember the moment more clearly. It didn't mean all that much to her. There was Curt there, in his tank top...

That's when I got the idea for this painting, says Harry. That's when it all got focused. I thought, if I could capture that flicker, that sense of aliveness in the midst of danger, I thought if I could capture that...

He holds a hand up in the air as if he's holding up a substantial thing, then his hand collapses back into his lap.

Most of my subjects don't ever show me that stuff, he says, still more or less to himself. Most of them don't have it in them, maybe. He takes another slug of his beer. I wanted to capture it, he whispers. With one hand he reaches out again, as if trying to grasp something essential. That aliveness. That daring.

Lindsay wonders if he's more drunk than she thought. You saw all that in me?

Can't you *see* it? he says, excited, pointing with his bottle. It's *there,* I think. I captured it.

She looks again at the painting. It is a pretty good likeness, as far as she knows what she looks like. She looks pretty, that's what she's noticed before, and as long as she looked good she wasn't all that much concerned with it. It's so hard to react to a picture of yourself, she says.

Can't you see it? he whispers.

Lindsay looks at the painting again. For some reason she feels a little destabilized, as if her limbs are about to rearrange themselves. I guess there does seem to be some kind of urgency to it, she says.

My friend Gillian thinks you look valiant, says Harry, talking to the canvas. That's the word she used. Valiant.

Lindsay stares at the painting, shrinking into herself. I sure don't feel very valiant.

Well, Harry slurs, you are. He pushes himself to his feet and tilts toward the kitchen. Or at least you look it.

Lindsay looks after him, then lets her gaze travel over the photos spread out all around her. Michael with Taggart on the floor of the family room. At a café table in Tortola. Standing in a canoe, using the paddle as a guitar. Always antic. She picks up a black-and-white picture of him sitting on the edge of a bed, bare-chested, a half-smile on his lips. Where did this one come from? she calls.

Harry comes back from the kitchen with a new bottle of beer. I don't know, he says. It was in the packet your mother sent.

She turns it over, no information, then looks at it again. I've never seen it before.

Harry sits next to her again, drawing the picture closer. Oh, he says. This one. I really like this one. He's such a heart-throb in this picture. He looks at Lindsay. Is it OK if I call your brother a heart-throb?

Harry, she says. You're drunk.

I suppose I am, he says. He looks back at the picture, then takes it from her. I think he's just made love, in this picture. Or he's about to make love. With whoever took the picture.

Lindsay takes the picture back again, looking at it with fresh eyes. He does look pretty happy.

But in a quieter way than in most of the other pictures, says Harry, leaning against her shoulder. Somehow it seems less *performed* here.

She gazes into the photo. Yeah. You can see his sadness here too. It's really kind of amazing when you look at it, how it captures both those things. The happiness and the sadness, under.

They study the photo together.

It seems like a very still moment, Harry murmurs. Between one thing and another. Like he's balanced between those two parts of himself.

Hmm, says Lindsay, nodding. It's so interesting to see a photo of Michael I haven't seen before. Most of the photos we had of him, there are stories to them, you know? You know where they were taken and what was going on. But there's something mysterious about this one. It gives you the feeling that he had a life apart from the rest of us. She holds the photo out at arm's length. This is Michael, apart. This is Michael, private. She lowers the picture to her lap and gazes down at it. Yeah, she murmurs, I like this picture.

23

Three AM and Harry is awake, staring into the dark. At first he tried to fight off the waking, squeezing his eyes as if to keep the sleep from seeping out, but in the end there was no winning, so he rolled on his back and opened his eyes. And now, as if it's coalescing out of the silence and darkness itself, it simply comes to him. An idea, out of nowhere, nudging its way into his mind like a self-important person might elbow his way onto an elevator. And once it has entered his mind, it moves center stage: a sudden vision of what this painting might become.

The more he stares at the thought, lying in bed in the dark in the night, the more the idea begins to shine, and the more he feels the clench in his stomach give and start to ease. He knows better than to jump up and run to his canvas, or even his sketchbook. He knows to leave the idea alone, to see if it will stay. And so he just lies there and looks at it until finally he falls back asleep.

The next morning Harry goes to the gym and stops for breakfast on the way home, just as he does every morning, all the while pretending he hasn't had an idea at all, all the while pretending he wasn't even in need of one. But he keeps it in his peripheral vision, watching to see if it's still there, watching to see if it stays, and it does. It hangs around him like a dog who's looking for a handout, until finally Harry turns and faces it squarely and makes his pact with it.

It feels like a reunion, embracing this new idea, like he has come back to something familiar, something that had always been there, something he's been staring at ever since he began the painting but never managed to see before. He hurries back to his studio, drops his gym bag by the couch and slides in behind his easel like a pilot sliding into the cockpit. His instruments are all around him—the tubes of pigment, the palette, the brushes, the little vanity mirror he uses to look at the painting backwards—everything he needs within reach, his own perfected little world.

He takes a deep breath to settle himself, and then with a prayer he begins. He works slowly, carefully, painstakingly, fitting the new in beside the old. It's like surgery—delicate, precise—and he works at it long, long hours, for days, thinking of nothing but paint and painting. He goes through packs of cigarettes, letting most of them burn in the ashtray after he's taken one or two puffs. The music runs out and he works in silence for long stretches without even knowing it. It makes him feel alive again, purposeful again. He has work to do and he's doing it. He doesn't know if it will pan out but at least he's back in the game again, and something wants him to succeed. There is a strength here, beside him, within him. All he has to do is open himself to it, and keep himself open to it, and soon enough he feels it there, like a follow-boat sliding in behind him, watching his progress, wishing him well, wishing him god speed.

And then, on the Tuesday before Thanksgiving, it's done. He steps back from it and knows it's done. It still needs to be drawn up to the surface, but there's nothing more to do until the client looks at it. That's how he thinks about all his paintings, as if they're dimly perceived images submerged far under water and his job is to draw them up, slowly, slowly, the way you bring a diver up from the depths, slowly making the image clearer and clearer until it finally breaks the surface and arrives in the world, fully realized, fully seen, fully clarified. That's the process, every time. Sometimes, of course, his cables break and the image falls back into the depths, never to be retrieved. All those paintings of Eric, for instance. But this one is still coming closer. There's more work to be done on it but it's close enough to the surface for them to see, and make their judgment. If they judge well, he can bring it on up. He knows, if they approve, he can bring it the rest of the way. The question is whether they will approve.

He sends Marjorie an email telling her he's changed the painting some, but he doesn't tell her just how. Better to have her see the new version in person, he decides, where he can be there to explain why he's done what he's done. But he sends her the message to prime her for it, so it won't be a total shock.

He thinks to ask Gillian to come and see it, but she's flat out on deadline herself, getting ready for her show. It occurs to him to call Lindsay, then, but then he thinks better of it. A part of him does want her to see it before her parents do, a part of him wants to enlist her help in selling this idea to them. But what if *she* doesn't like it? *Then* how will he present it? He doesn't want to give her the chance to shake his confidence, so he decides to wait and do it all at once. Just take the plunge all at once.

He wishes he had someone to share all this with—the anxiety, the triumph (if it is to be a triumph), the wait. He remembers when Eric was around, they'd always talk about his paintings. Not at length—Eric didn't know much about painting—but he was in and out of Harry's studio all the time, aware of the progress, or lack of it. He was part of the process, just by being close by. But there isn't anybody close by. So

Harry goes to the movies. He rents videos. He takes walks. He takes himself out to dinner and drinks wine and reads magazines. He waits, and chews at his hangnails, staring out at the endless rush of traffic on the turnpike, wondering where it is that everybody's in such a hurry to get to.

24

David is standing at the kitchen table, shuffling through the mail, when Marjorie appears in the doorway and asks him what he's doing home. She doesn't say, he notes, What are you doing home so early? She says What are you doing home? As if he doesn't belong here, as if she doesn't want him here. At least that's how it sounds to him.

I left the office early, he says. To run some errands.

She doesn't say anything but she doesn't leave, either. She just stands there in the doorway like a sergeant-at-arms, silently demanding that he say more. As if she doesn't even have to state her wishes aloud; she just imposes them by her royal presence. He sets down his briefcase and stares at it a moment, sharpening his sword. Then he looks at her and takes his aim. I was looking at a condo, he says.

A condo?

Yeah, a condo.

She stares at him. Why?

I'm thinking, he says, maybe I should move out for a while.

He watches the information course through her, setting off signals here and there, memories, worries, questions.

Move out, she repeats, robotically.

He keeps his gaze trained on her, intense, to drive his intention home. I'm thinking it might be better for us if we lived apart for a while.

For a while? she says. What does that mean?

I don't know, he says. A few months. A year. We'd have to see how it goes.

How it goes?

It's almost comical, David thinks. All she can do is parrot back whatever he says, as a question. But he doesn't really feel like laughing.

Marjorie pulls out a chair and sits. She looks at his briefcase, then up at him. How long have you been thinking this?

I've been wondering for a while.

I thought you were thinking about a house, she says. For us. Not a condo for yourself.

I guess I've changed my thinking on that.

Marjorie looks around as if she is trying to find some meaning somewhere. The cookie jar? The blender? Dishwasher?

Look, says David. He sits and leans across the table. Marjorie. Look at me. She does. You and I haven't been getting along real well in the past few months...

Well we've had a lot to deal with, here. You expect us just to cruise along as if nothing has happened? And now you're going to walk out on me and leave me all alone here?

David slumps back in his chair, looks down at his hands in his lap. He doesn't have the heart for this. He doesn't really want to hurt her, he doesn't want them to hurt each other. Which is exactly why he's thinking to leave.

He takes a deep breath and lets it out slowly. I guess I just feel like I need to be alone for a while. I don't feel comfortable here. I don't feel comfortable with you, I don't feel comfortable with myself. I just...I just think a new place might help.

A new place alone. Without me.

He nods. I think it might be best.

Marjorie stares at him a moment, then stands and goes to the window, leaning against the counter, looking out. Where's the condo? she says at last.

Mount Adams.

Mount Adams, she snorts. Of course. How big?

Two bedrooms, with a study.

Does it have a view of the river?

Yes.

She nods, still gazing out the window.

I didn't buy it, he says. I just looked.

She turns to him. Are you going to?

He looks up at her. I don't know. He finds it sadly satisfying that he has shaken her up this much. He's managed to hit her back, as hard as she'd hit him, but he doesn't feel good about it.

I can't live like this, Marjorie, he says. Feeling like a criminal in my own house.

She leans toward him. Why in the world do you feel like a *criminal?*

He lets his gaze settle on the stack of mail on the table before him, as if it might intervene here, as if it might answer for him.

Well, he says at last, standing. You should have the answer to that.

He looks at her. She searches his eyes, trying to find some other answer there than the one he's giving her.

Lola got us tickets for Boston, he says. And we've got a room at the Ritz. Did you talk with Lindsay?

Yes.

He nods. His gaze goes wide-eyed, dazed. He feels himself soften a little. I guess I'll go change, he says quietly.

25

L indsay does not want to do this.

She slapped the snooze alarm four or five times before getting up this morning. She took an extra-long shower and lingered over a second cup of coffee while watching the Macy's Parade. She tried on three different outfits before finally settling on the first one. But finally she couldn't delay any longer.

So here she is now, standing at the door to her parents' hotel room, head bowed, centering herself the way she's been taught to do before she enters the stage.

She lifts her chin, and knocks. There is a rustle of sudden movement, then the door swings open and the space is flooded with her mother's excitement and need.

Lindsay! she cries. How *are* you?

Her mother looks perfectly put together, as always. Wool and cashmere, lustrous hair, understated gold. She envelops Lindsay in a hug—her smell is sweet and familiar, and her hair tickles Lindsay's nose—then she steps back and holds Lindsay at arm's length.

Honey, she purrs. You look wonderful.

Thanks, says Lindsay. So do you.

She steps past her mother and finds her father in the middle of the room, looking oddly out of place and adrift, waiting for her to come to him. She goes to him and gives him a hug and he holds her a little longer—quite a lot longer—than she is accustomed to.

Let me take this, says Marjorie, pulling Lindsay's coat off her shoulders and holding it at arm's length. I think it's time we got you a new one, she mutters, brushing imaginary lint before she tosses it over a chair.

So! she says, turning back to Lindsay and brightening, clapping her hands. Sit down! Tell us everything!

Lindsay moves to the desk but her mother insists she take the wingback chair. Then she sits at the desk herself, perched on the edge of her seat as if she's about to start taking notes. Her father settles himself on the couch with a scotch. It's only noon.

So tell us! says Marjorie. How is it going? We can't *wait* to see this show! We've been telling everybody about it.

And here it is already, even sooner than Lindsay had expected. She takes a deep breath. I quit, she says.

Marjorie almost misses a beat but then plows on as if she hasn't heard. Your Aunt Lee and Uncle Steve are coming, and I think the boys are coming too, if they're home from school in time. The Whitmores are even thinking of coming because they're going to be out in Springfield...Laura's mother isn't doing well...

Lindsay watches, dumbfounded, as her mother spins on, out of control.

What did you say? says David.

She turns to him. I quit the show.

Now Marjorie stops and looks at her. She seems to have trouble determining exactly what species Lindsay is. What do you mean, you quit the show?

I quit, says Lindsay. I dropped out. She tries to make it sound casual. They were going to replace me anyway.

I don't understand, says Marjorie. She says it the way she would speak to a plumber who's failed to fix the toilet; it is an accusation. What does that mean, dropped out?

It means I'm not in the show.

Marjorie stares at her. You don't just quit, she says at last, tight-lipped.

I did.

But *why?*

I'm *tired.*

Well *everybody* gets *tired,* says Marjorie. How do you expect to do eight shows a week without getting tired? Of course you're tired. But you're a professional!

I'm not a professional.

Well you won't be at this rate, she mutters, shifting her weight in her chair. Then she shifts it back and leans toward Lindsay. What do you think you're doing? This is a great opportunity for you. Everybody's talking about it. Your aunt and uncle are coming to see you, the Whitmores are coming to see you...

I don't care about the Whitmores.

Marjorie draws back, indignant, squints her eyes at her daughter. Davenports do not quit, she says evenly.

Lindsay settles into herself, cocks her head and returns the stare. Michael did, she says. Didn't he?

Marjorie gapes at her. Her eye begins to twitch. She stands and turns to walk away, turns back, then turns away again. She looks like a robot with a short circuit, deconstructing before Lindsay's eyes.

Mom, Lindsay pleads. Please understand. I just couldn't do it anymore. I couldn't keep going like nothing was wrong.

Marjorie turns on her. What other choice do we have? she whispers. Her voice is ferocious and desperate, tight. What other choice do you think we have?

Lindsay stares at her a long, sad moment. I don't know, she says at last, looking down. I just feel like I need to stop for a while. Maybe if I can just stop singing and dancing for a while I'll come up with an answer to that question.

David stirs from his silence. He stands and goes to Lindsay, drawing her to her feet and putting his arms around her. It's OK, he murmurs, rocking her. You do whatever you need to do.

She rests her head lightly on his chest. He smells of scotch; it's only noon. She looks up at her mother, standing across the room in front of the mirror. She can see her face in the reflection, struggling for composure.

Mom? she says, holding out her arm, inviting her to join them.

Marjorie cuts her eyes to Lindsay, then takes a deep breath and straightens her back and returns her gaze to her own reflection, twisting her wedding ring.

26

Harry mashes out his cigarette and paces, tending to tiny things. Straightening stacks of books he's already straightened several times before. Changing the music from Mozart to Bach. Moving the pastries from plate to platter, glancing now and again at the canvas to see if it still looks right to him. Every time he looks, it looks fine, but he can't help looking again, then again, like a stage mother fussing over her child just before an audition.

Harry is always anxious at unveilings, but this is a different order of business. He understands what Marjorie Davenport wanted from this painting and he knows she isn't going to get it, so he's far more nervous than usual. And he's nervous for Lindsay too. He cares what she thinks about it, maybe even more than what her mother thinks. And the father is a total wild card, Harry doesn't know what to expect from him. But Harry is a professional. He's been through this scene many times and he knows what to do.

He lights another cigarette.

Finally, ten minutes late, the bell rings. He hurries to buzz them in, then drapes a sheet over his easel. He mounts the steps two at a time and pauses on the balcony to see that everything is in place, then he turns toward the elevator.

The lift arrives, the gate slides back, the door opens into the hall. First comes Lindsay, smiling at him, in jeans and a jersey, her jacket open. She gives him a wary, probing look, as if to ask how to play this scene. Behind her comes the mother, smiling. Just as handsome as he remembers, just as perfectly groomed, but she seems a little tense and brittle. Harry doesn't have time to assess it, though, because behind them, now, comes the man, the father. David? Christ. Harry has a moment of panic. Does he have the name right? Is it David? Whatever it is, he looks pretty corporate, even in a V-neck sweater. Maybe it's the dress coat.

Hi Harry, says Lindsay. She takes his hand in both of hers. You remember my mother, she says as Marjorie arrives behind her, holding out her hand.

Mr. Garrett! says Marjorie, a little too brightly. She turns to the man. This is my husband, David.

Harry shakes the husband's hand, thinking David. Yes, it's David. David. Then he steps aside, gesturing to the door, and Lindsay leads the way as if this studio is her turf. Harry appreciates the effect: if she is relaxed and comfortable here, it will help put her parents at ease. He follows them down the stairs to the studio floor, where they cluster near the couch— his audience, his patrons, his judges.

Did you have a nice Thanksgiving? he asks, arriving on the floor behind them. Are you comfortably settled? They sing out their praises of Duxbury and their arrangement at the Ritz.

Ah, says Harry. The Ritz. Did you know there were once three kings in the barbershop there? All getting their hair cut at the same time. Entirely by chance. Three kings.

Which three kings?

I haven't a clue.

He gets them seated around the old trunk and brings out the coffee and pastry—apologizing, in a self-mocking way, that it isn't up to the fare at the Ritz—and as they chat, Harry becomes increasingly aware of the three of them as a family. He has never seen Lindsay and her mother in each other's company before, has never seen the father at all. Now here they all are, the three of them, a little world unto themselves.

He can see that Lindsay has her father's eyes. That Michael has his mouth, had his mouth. And looking at the three of them here, he feels that he is inside these people in a peculiar way. That he is a part of their family, or at least that he has gained entrance to it. Like a housekeeper, familiar with all their details but not quite a part of them. It is a strange, unauthorized feeling.

Finally Marjorie can't wait any longer. When do we get to see it? she says, sitting up on the edge of the couch, clasping her hands in her lap.

It's that elephant over there, says Lindsay. Underneath the sheet. He was hoping we wouldn't notice.

Just building anticipation, jokes Harry. He hunches forward a little bit. Let me start by saying a few things.

They all lean toward him, or he feels that they do.

He clears his throat, staring at his shoes, then fixes his gaze on the mother. As I told you in my email, he says, the painting has changed some since you last saw it. You know I felt it really wasn't working the way we had it.

Marjorie gives him a tentative nod.

Of course I didn't want to believe it, he says, rushing past this moment. I wanted to believe it could work. But I felt all along there was something fundamentally *wrong* with it. And the longer I worked on it, the more convinced I became that it had to change.

They all just sit there, staring at him. He wants them to nod, he wants them to smile. He wants them to murmur assurances. But they just sit there staring at him. It is time to cut to the chase. Stand up, Harry, he tells himself.

Now move to the easel. Remove the sheet.

Turn the easel, first ninety degrees. Position yourself and step back.

Now then. Complete the turn.

Harry watches as the three faces reveal their reaction to what he's shown them. It seems to him their jaws all drop at once, but it doesn't actually happen. It's more like their faces just fall open, like gates swinging open in the wind.

Lindsay looks at the painting with a strange half-smile on her face. She seems interested in it, intrigued, and Harry takes that as a good sign. Her father seems to be curious—not at the change in the painting, it seems to Harry, but in the image itself. As if he finds something in it that is meaningful to him, or might be, if he could figure it out. Another encouraging sign. But the mother's reaction is troubling. Harry can feel her recoiling inside, like a leaf drying up and turning to dust.

I don't understand, she says at last.

Harry takes a long deep breath, then moves away from his shelter behind the painting and positions himself to the side, halfway between the canvas and the family, to act as mediator. He turns to look at the picture. There is Lindsay, as before, seated on the piano bench, all vulnerability and strength. But behind her now, instead of shadows with Michael emerging from them, a wall has been revealed, moss green. It is dim, it is still in shadow, but it is there—there is no longer the sense of a bottomless dark behind her. She is contained; she is *backed up*. And on the wall behind her there is now a portrait of Michael, a painting within a painting, hanging in a golden frame.

Why did you change it? Marjorie whispers.

Harry turns to her. He glances at Lindsay for moral support but she is just watching him, curious to hear his explanation too.

He takes a step toward them. All the time I was painting this, he says, I had the feeling Michael was fighting me. That he didn't.... How can I put this? That he didn't want to be represented this way, the way we had him. But before I made the decision to change it, I asked Lindsay to look at it. Just to test out my feeling about it. And her reaction convinced me I was right.

David and Marjorie look at Lindsay.

She said it made her feel threatened, says Harry.

Lindsay? says Marjorie.

I thought it was *me*, she says. Not the painting.

No, says Harry. I think it *was* the painting. *Something* about the painting. Something *I* put in the painting.

Marjorie looks at the canvas again, then shakes her head as if to clear it and abruptly stands. Would you excuse me a moment? she says. Could you direct me to the bathroom?

Harry steps toward the kitchen, gesturing to the back. The switch is on the outside, he says, but she doesn't respond. He turns back to Lindsay and David.

The painting is *good*, says David. It is. He seems full of intention, saying that. He glances at Lindsay. I like the strength he's captured in you. He looks at Harry. You've really brought that out.

It's stronger now than it was, Harry says. The way we had it before, it was more about her vulnerability. But with Michael contained in that frame, now...

He glances at Lindsay but she doesn't seem to hear him. She is staring at the painting now with a sudden recognition. It's that photograph, she says. She looks at Harry. Isn't it? That photograph we were looking at.

What picture is that? says David.

There was this photo, says Lindsay, in among the photos Mom sent, of Michael sitting on a bed. He didn't have a shirt on. Harry thought...Harry thought he looked happy, there. Mom didn't know who took the picture.

Harry returns to his painting corner, unpins the photo and takes it to David.

Oh, David says. This one, yeah. His roommate took this picture. He gave it to me when I went to see him, after Michael died.

His roommate took it?

Yeah, says David. He was kind of a shutterbug.

Lindsay looks at Harry, a curious smile on her face. You sure about that? she says to her father, her eyes still fixed on Harry.

Yeah, says David. Certain.

Marjorie returns from the bathroom, a little unsteady on her feet, the color gone from her face. She settles herself on the couch again and David leans toward her. Look at what he's done with Lindsay, he says. Hasn't he captured her, here? Look at her eyes. Is that our Lindsay, or what?

Marjorie nods, a little numbly.

I like what's happening between us, says Lindsay. In there, in the space between us. She gets up and goes to the canvas, to point out what she means. She traces the negative space between her shoulder and the frame of Michael's portrait, as if it were a solid shape. In here, she says. This darkness, with this glow of light from the left. I don't know why, but I like it. And the highlight on my earring, here.

And the hair, says David. You feel like you could touch it.

They continue talking for more than half an hour—Is my nose really that big? says Lindsay; Is there something off in her mouth? says David; Were Michael's ears that low? says

Lindsay—but during that time Marjorie doesn't say much of anything. She listens to David and Lindsay, looking at them dumbly as if they are speaking another language, then she looks at the painting again, then at Lindsay and David again. She seems to Harry like a child watching grown-ups argue her future.

Mrs. Davenport? he says at last, inviting her to comment.

She glances at him, then back at the painting. They're very good likenesses, she says.

He nods and smiles, encouraging her to go on but instead she glances at her watch. I think we ought to go, she says. She looks at Lindsay, then David. If we mean to get to Rockport today...

Oh, says Lindsay, surprised. Well OK.

OK, says David. Sure.

They stand, then Harry rises too, disturbed by the abruptness of this. Is that all he's going to get from her? Is that all she's going to say? They move to the stairs and he follows them up, making arrangements for them to come for a second viewing the next day, but still the mother has nothing to say. Harry is beside himself, wondering what to do with her.

When they reach the lift, he shakes David's hand and Lindsay gives him a peck on the cheek, then he turns to Marjorie, takes her hand.

It's kind of a shock, isn't it? he says softly. To see the painting life-size.

Her only reaction: a twitch of the mouth.

Even when it's the picture they've been seeing all along, says Harry, people are always shocked to see the image finally fixed. So to see something different from what you expected...

She nods curtly, cutting him off. You're a very skilled painter, Mr. Garrett, she says. They're very good likenesses.

Then the lift arrives and she turns to it. David glances at Harry briefly, then opens the door and follows the others in, sliding the gate shut. He gives Harry a gaze of firm intention. We'll see you tomorrow, he says.

Harry nods and closes the door, then listens as the lift descends.

Christ, she fucking hated it. Is she even going to accept it, pay him the rest of his fee? Well the father seems convinced—he was even talking delivery dates—so it seems he'll get his fee. And Lindsay seemed to like it, even though she hated the whole idea from the start. So on some counts the painting is a success. Two-thirds of a success.

But Jesus, the mother. He's had some bad reactions at unveilings before. One woman even accepted the painting, paid him, then took it home and burned it. But this. She was just fucking catatonic. She acted like she'd been hit on the head with a brick. And that she blamed him for it.

Well, he knew he was taking a risk to make such a dramatic change without consulting her. Why the hell didn't he consult her? Why didn't he tell her what he was up to? Of *course* she was going to hate it. Even if she didn't hate the change, she'd hate the fact he just went ahead and did it without consulting her. What the hell was he thinking?

But as soon as he asks the question, he knows the answer. He didn't consult her because he was scared she wouldn't agree to it, because he was scared she'd stop him. And he had his own agenda here. He needed to change it for himself, and for Lindsay.

Something had to move.

PART IV

27

At first it is just a presence that Marjorie can only sense, the way one might sense the presence of another person in a dark room.

It announces itself on Sunday morning, the anniversary of Michael's death, as she sits in church with Lindsay and David. She's aware of it still there after church, when David and Lindsay go to have another look at the painting. She feels it grow more definite as she packs for the trip home, as David and Lindsay return with the news they've arranged the final sitting. She's aware of it gaining strength in the taxi, aware of it becoming a pressure within her as the plane lifts off, but it isn't until she actually speaks the words that she understands what it is.

I don't want that painting, she says.

David looks at her. What?

She keeps her eyes on the seatback in front of her. I said I don't want that painting.

David turns toward her. What do you mean you don't want the painting?

I mean I don't want that painting, she says again, turning to look at her husband. That is not the painting I commissioned. That is not the painting I want.

But he's done a wonderful job, says David. They're amazing likenesses.

I don't like it. It looks stupid, that painting hanging on the wall behind Lindsay. That painting doesn't even exist. How could it be hanging on the wall behind her? It doesn't even exist.

It exists in the painting.

It's a stupid trick. The guy is a hack.

No he's not, says David, offended now. Just look what he did with Lindsay, alone. If you don't even look at Michael, if you just look at Lindsay, it's worth the price.

Marjorie shakes her head. What kind of business dealing is that? she says, getting more upset the more she talks. Just changing the thing that we'd agreed on? If I did that to a client, I'd be fried. Fried. *Oh, you want a red chair? Well here's a green one. The red chair didn't* speak *to me.* If you did that, you'd be fired on the spot. You want Ivory? No, here's Borax. It's ridiculous. Absolutely ridiculous.

But I *like* it the way it is.

She looks at him, exasperated, then throws her hands in the air. *Now* you like it!

What's that mean?

It means I've been trying to get you interested in this painting all fall. I commissioned this painting for *both* of us, for all three of us. I thought it would be *good* for us! I thought it might *help* us! But you, you couldn't be interested. All you could do was sit in your chair and stare at the television set, sucking down your scotch.

That's not fair.

No it's not! I've been trying to help us! I've been trying to *do* something! And you just couldn't be bothered! You're right! There's nothing fair in that!

Marjorie...

Now all of a sudden you're interested! Now all of a sudden you want it!

And what's so wrong with that?

Marjorie turns away, disgusted.

David takes a deep breath and stares at his hands, calming himself. Look, he says evenly, still staring at his hands. I know how hard this is. It's like Garrett was saying, the image is so final. Lindsay will grow beyond this moment, we'll always have a new version of her, but to some extent this image will be the Michael we live with the rest of our lives. It's hard to settle for that.

I don't *want* that image of Michael, she hisses, turning back to him, her eyes suddenly filling with tears. I don't want an *image* of Michael!

David fixes her with a cold stare. Then why did you commission a painting?

Marjorie catches her breath and glares at him, shocked. Then a muffled sob escapes from her throat and she looks away.

If you had any idea, David mutters. If you had any idea, the image I carry around of Michael. If you had the slightest fucking idea what I see when I close my eyes at night...

Marjorie stares at the window shade, the small plastic handle for pulling it down, absolutely frozen. Finally she turns back to him and he meets her gaze. She has never seen this look in his eyes before. It is the look she saw in the eyes of the boys who came back from Vietnam—glazed, red, dazed, the life knocked out of them. His eyes look so old in this moment, so ancient, she'd swear she can see fires burning in them, back behind the darkness. It leaves her speechless, silenced.

If you don't want it, he says quietly, then maybe I'll just take it with me.

She stares at him, slowly absorbing his meaning. Then she feels a thump in the belly of the plane, as if the landing gear has just been stowed, and turns quickly away from him, to the window. It is dark, rain is lashing the glass, streaming backward in the wind, leaving beads of silver in its wake. She watches the light at the tip of the wing, blinking on and off, her mind spinning out of gear. The only thought that comes to her is that *Twilight Zone* episode where a passenger sees a monster crawling on the wing outside his window, but no one will believe him.

28

Lindsay is surprised. Somehow she thought all Dartmouth men would be burly and muscular, football players and frat boys—even though, of course, Michael was neither of those—but this guy Jason is perplexing. He not only doesn't fit that mold, he doesn't seem to fit any mold. He seems to be two people in one. One minute you look at him and he's just a regular guy, and kind of a cute one, at that. Bright warm eyes, rosy cheeks, quick smile, sensuous lips. But the next time you look, he's gone all geek—recessive chin, too-big nose and a really unfortunate hairline. When she glances away she doesn't know who will be there when she looks back, the regular guy or the geek. But that, of course, is why she's driven all the way up here in the snow, to find out who Jason is.

I'm sorry to bother you, she says. In the middle of exams and everything.

Not a problem, says Jason, setting his Coke and fries on the table and slipping his empty tray onto the chair beside him. I'm always glad to have an excuse to take a study break. He glances up. Hey Wes, he says to a guy squeezing by their table; the café is crowded today. He looks back at Lindsay. See? *Everybody's* taking a break.

Lindsay watches him salt his fries and dump a dollop of ketchup into the corner of the basket. She sips her Coke and sets it down, waits for Jason to look at her. I just wanted to meet you, she says when his eyes finally meet hers.

It's good to meet *you,* he says, nudging the fries toward her. Michael told me a lot about you.

Lindsay looks at the fries and smiles, wondering how to respond to that. It's not exactly a compliment, so it doesn't really require any thanks. She decides just to let it pass and move right on to why she's come. It's been a year now since Michael died, she says.

Yeah, Jason murmurs quietly.

And we're still...I'm still...I don't know. She glances around the room at the mounds of coats, the steaming cups, the stacks of books, the huddled couples. Things almost feel worse this year, she says, than they did last year. She looks at Jason. You know? The shock has sort of worn off and we're just left with this gaping hole in our lives.

I know, he says, leaning back. I mean, I don't know. But I can imagine.

Lindsay is encouraged by this. He seems to be open to discussion. Did you...? she says, leaning toward him. Were you and Michael very close?

Well, we lived together.

For a year, she says. Right? Freshman year, and then again sophomore year?

Right.

Was he...? Did he ever...? She twists her hands. I know you already talked to my dad. But I just have to ask you. For myself, you know?

He nods, a concerned look in his eyes.

Lindsay leans forward over her hands, as if she has a stomach ache. And she does, in fact, she realizes, have a stomach ache. Did you and Michael...she begins. She stares at the fries. How to say this? She looks up at Jason. He's watching her, waiting. Did you and Michael ever have...like...anything going?

Jason frowns and cocks his head, tipping his chair onto its back legs.

I'm sorry, says Lindsay, sitting back, flustered. I didn't... She glances away then leans across the table to Jason again. Did you and Michael have an affair?

Jason's chair slams down onto all four legs and his face falls open in disbelief.

I'm sorry, says Lindsay. I'm sorry, I'm sorry. She waves her hands in the air to erase what she's just said. I know that's a really.... She plants her hands at her temples. I know that's a really *invasive* question. But I'm just trying to figure out....

I'm not that way, says Jason. It seems to be just a statement of fact; he doesn't seem to have taken offense.

Lindsay lowers her hands and looks up. Was Michael?

I don't know, says Jason. I don't think so. He never made a pass at me. Why? What makes you ask?

Well there's this picture you took of him, she says. She rummages in her bag, pulls out the photo she borrowed from Harry and slides it across the table to him. You gave it to my dad, I guess.

Jason looks down at the photo without picking it up. Yeah, I remember that picture.

Lindsay twists her hands in her lap, rocking back and forth. This feels so silly to say, she mutters. But see there's this guy who's painting this picture, this portrait of me and Michael. My mother commissioned it. And he's using this picture as the model for Michael. Because of the look in his eyes. He said he thinks that in that picture Michael looks like he's in love. And it's true. You know? Isn't it? Just look. There *is* something in his eyes, in that picture. Some kind of...I don't know, *something* warm. And so Harry was speculating.... Lindsay looks at Jason then tosses her hands in the air, giving up. Harry was speculating that maybe Michael was in love with whoever took the picture. And then we found out *you* took the picture…

Jason watches her, wary, and Lindsay realizes how idiotic all this must sound to him. Well I started wondering, she blurts out, rushing on in desperation. I mean, if Michael was gay, maybe that would help to explain…. You see? If he were gay, if he were in love with you and maybe couldn't deal with that…. She stops, as if at the edge of a cliff, and looks at Jason again, aware of just how ridiculous she seems. *I don't know!* she bursts out, angry. *I don't know!* Suddenly she is in tears, blubbering. I'm sorry. I know it's silly. I shouldn't have come here. This is ridiculous.

No, says Jason. It's OK. He reaches across the table as if to take her hand. I'm glad you came, he says. 'Cause I lost Michael too, you know.

She nods.

And if I could help you find the answer, I would. But Michael and I…. He shakes his head apologetically. We were roommates, that's all.

She looks up at him and nods, then bursts into tears again.

Jason pulls his hand back and waits for her tears to subside. I don't think Michael was gay, he says at last. And I sure don't think he was in love with me. But I don't think any of us knew him very well, you know? He was a very private guy. I mean, he was always friendly and funny and everybody liked him. But you never really knew what was going on with him. Sometimes I got the feeling people just projected onto him whatever they wanted him to be. Sometimes I got the feeling that's what he wanted people to do. I *lived* with him but I didn't know him. I don't think any of us did. Obviously, none of us did. If we had, we might have stopped him.

Lindsay watches him, drinking him in. No one has ever talked to her about Michael in quite this way before.

I'm sorry, Jason laughs. I never thought I'd be apologizing for not hooking up with some guy.

She laughs with him, using a napkin to wipe her eyes.

Jason studies her as she collects herself. He seems to be thinking of something. Then he sits back and gazes again at the photo. He looks at it for a long moment, then finally picks it up. I remember the night I took this, he says. We'd been sitting around, just shootin the shit. Drinking tequila, I think. It was about two in the morning, I was fooling around with my new camera. We'd been talking about our lives back home. I'd been telling him about my family, about my brothers and sisters. He lifts his eyes to look at Lindsay over the top of the picture. He was telling me about you.

Lindsay looks up, breath stopped.

That's the look you see in his eyes, says Jason. He was talking about you.

29

Marjorie rinses her coffee cup, then looks out at the backyard. It is a beautiful day for December, sunny and breezy. A brilliant blue sky with just a few wispy clouds. Leaves are still falling, even this late, from the yellow maple and the oaks. It would be so much simpler, she thinks, if the trees would let go of their leaves all at once, so people could rake them up and be done with it. But every year it's the same. They just refuse to give in to winter, holding on until the last moment.

She pulls a coat and hat from the closet and steps out onto the patio, then takes a rake from the garden shed and sets to work methodically, listening to the sound of the tines twanging against the ground, the crackle and swish of the leaves and twigs. She doesn't really need to do this, the yard service will do it, but it feels good to be outside smelling the leaves and listening to the crunch of the acorns under her feet.

A gust of wind picks up the leaves and scatters them back across the yard. She stops and sighs, then retraces her steps and begins again, raking a little faster now to stay ahead of the wind. But the wind, as if it is playing a game, swirls the leaves across the lawn once more. Marjorie flaps her arms in exasperation, then plunges back in and rakes faster. But the faster she rakes, the harder it blows. She rakes faster and faster, harder and harder, but the wind will not relent and finally she throws the rake into the wind as if she could stop it that way.

Stop! she cries. Just *stop!*

But the rake just lands with a twang. She stands there staring at it, her shoulders slumped, then finally drags the rake back to the shed and seats herself on the garden wall. Her anger deflates, absurd as it is. And then she seems to keep on deflating. The anger leaves her, the frustration, and then it seems her very breath leaves her and she is just a husk on the wall, to be blown away by winter wind.

It all came out over dinner last night. David is making plans to move after the first of the year. He has been thinking a lot about this. Buying a condo was too big a step, so now he's planning on renting. He's got a realtor working on it. He actually has a *plan*.

She sighs and looks up at the trees, the maple and the oaks. She admires their tenacity, as if they could stop the cycle of the seasons by the sheer force of their will. She finds herself looking toward the woods out back and thinking about the will to hold on. Where does it come from? she wonders. And where does it go? What is it that makes something want to *stop* holding on?

Gradually her gaze narrows in on the gate in the fence by the woods, and she feels something settle inside herself. It settles into her the way that leaf settled onto the wall beside her. The knowledge of what she has to do.

She pushes herself to her feet and starts to walk toward the woods. Her legs seem to move of their own accord, as if she is being reeled in. She reaches the gate and unlatches it. Ah, she remembers this latch. She hasn't worked it for over a year. But she remembers it now, its simple efficiency. She closes the gate behind her, stands leaning against it with her hands behind her. Then she begins to pick her way forward, down the path, past the brambles, past the pet cemetery, past the compost heap, until the little stable comes into view. The little red stable with its corral, where the kids kept their pony when they were young.

She comes to the edge of the clearing and stops. Can she really go through with this? Does she have any choice, at this point? There is nothing left to do. She knows, in this moment, that is the truth: there is nothing left to do. Nothing else she does can matter, unless she does this too.

She takes a step forward, then another. She has a weightless feeling now, as if she is turning into water, or air. It isn't unpleasant. In fact there is something distinctly *her* about it, something distinctly Marjorie. It is Marjorie, here, who feels like water. Marjorie, like air. She is nowhere else, no one else is here.

She curves around to the left of the stable, past the old wagon wheel, toward the narrower clearing in back. She creeps to the edge of the building. Then she steps around the corner to look at the boulder that Michael sat on, the boulder where David found him. The sight of it knocks the wind out of her, and she has to gasp for air. She has seen this boulder hundreds of times, but not since Michael ended his life there. It looks to her now like an electric chair, an instrument of death—so inert, so lacking intention, but somehow evil in its very existence.

The wind kicks up in the trees above her and she looks up at the waving branches. She imagines they are waving at her, trying to warn her away from this place, but her feet seem to have grown roots. She leans against the stable, staring up at the trees, and concentrates on getting air back into her lungs. I can do this, she thinks. I can do this. She stares at the sky for several minutes, stabilizing herself. Then she closes her eyes and lowers her head. She concentrates on her breathing, eyes closed, then opens her eyes and looks at the leaves and brambles at her feet. Slowly she lifts her gaze until she is looking again at the boulder.

She takes a step toward it, then another, moving toward it deliberately, the way a hunter might approach prey he isn't sure he's killed, a muscular terrified animal who might suddenly attack. She pulls up next to it and stands looking down on it. It is just a common boulder, unremarkable as dirt, but on the far side there is a dark smear that Marjorie imagines is a bloodstain. She takes a deep breath, then another. Then she stoops and places her hands on the boulder. She can't believe she's doing this. She's actually *touching* it? But then, with her eyes squeezed shut, with her face contorted into a grimace, she turns and lowers herself onto the rock, sitting on it as Michael did.

The stone is cold as steel, it burns through the seat of her pants, but she wills herself to withstand it. She places her elbows on her knees, lowers her head into her hands and lets the cold come in. It stings at first, but she doesn't resist it. She concentrates on her breathing, on the darkness behind her eyelids, on the cool of her hands against her face. The protected cave she has made of her body. She concentrates on the swell of her belly as she breathes in and out, on the sound of the air moving in and out of her. She presses her fingertips to her temples and feels the pulse of her blood. She smells her fingertips: coffee.

She sits that way for a very long time, concentrating on the signs of life going on in her. And eventually, gradually, she feel ripples of warmth coming back to her, intermingling with the cold. Not battle so much as accommodation. Adjustment. It happens of its own accord. An automatic, natural response.

She stands, unsteady on her feet. She has to relay herself from tree to tree, to the side of the barn, for support while she walks. She leans against the barn for a while, as rubbery in the legs as if she'd just run a marathon, and just as pixilated in the mind. She breathes, and breathes. She listens to her breathing, to know that she is alive, still here.

She watches her feet walk her back to the house, crackling the leaves and sticks beneath them. She watches her hands unlatch the gate then latch it up again, and feels the rough, sturdy texture of the wood. She listens to the wind in the trees, lifts her face to its cool touch, traces its coursing into her lungs. She sees her house, familiar, strange, as if it were her childhood home, long ago left behind. She stops at the door. Should she go in? A strange thought, but she wonders. It's as if she is in a dream: she knows this house is hers but she doesn't know if she's free to enter, or safe to enter. It seems dangerous as that rock, somehow.

She puts her hand on the door handle—metallic, cold— then backs away from the door and gently lowers herself into one of the wrought iron chairs on the patio. She sits there for some time, just looking, the way an invalid sits in the sunroom after an operation, looking at nothing, thinking of nothing, just letting the body do its work. It's a strangely comforting state to be in. This sense that something is going on inside over which she has no control, except that she can leave it alone, just stay out of its way. She sits there for quite a while, just watching. Just sitting. Then finally she pushes herself to her feet and goes into the house to make herself a cup of tea.

30

Harry leans against his door, waiting for the lift to arrive. He is looking forward to this visit and dreading it at the same time. He is eager to see Lindsay again, and to finish the painting, and to talk with her about her parents, and her parents' reaction, and how it was for her being with them, and how her finals are going and how she's feeling about going home for Christmas and what she thinks of the painting....

He can't quite remember the last time he felt so eager to see someone. It reminds him of the first day she came here, all his anxiety about it. This time it's more anticipation than anxiety, but there is an undeniable edge: he knows that after today he'll probably never see her again.

When she steps out of the lift, he is pleased to see she is wearing her hair the way it is in the painting. She's done her make-up and worn the earrings; she's even worn the little black dress. She didn't have to do that, and she knew she didn't have to do that, but she did it anyway. It makes Harry feel that this meeting is as important to her as it is to him. She's dressed up for their date: there's no guy who doesn't like to see that.

As she brushes by him to the studio, he catches a whiff of cold from the street, mixed with something sweet and spicy, just a hint of spring in the air. He follows her down the stairs, watching her as she drops her pack on the couch, removes her coat and looks around the room.

Gee, the place looks nice, she says.

Apropos of what, he isn't sure. Is she really noticing that he tidied up for her? It makes him feel, again, that she's paying as close attention to this as he is, and that feels good to him.

So, he says. What can I get you? Coffee? Tea? Cookies? Fruit? There's an ashtray. You want some juice? Some vodka?

Hey! she says. This is better than Starbuck's! How about tea and cookies.

While he's preparing to make the tea she opens her backpack and rummages, then joins him in the kitchen, perching on a stool. Thank you for this, she says, pushing an envelope across the counter.

Harry glances at it, recognizes it as the photo of Michael she borrowed from him. Aha, he says. So what did you learn?

She gives him a significant look, then slowly shakes her head. They were just roommates, she says, spreading her hands palms up.

Well, says Harry. I'm not surprised. Although he does recognize in himself the slightest bit of disappointment: a part of him would have liked to think that Michael was on his team, so to speak.

While he's pulling out the teacups and napkins and sugar and lemon, all that, Lindsay recounts the scene to him—the crowded café, the outrageous questions, her fit of tears and confusion. Harry listens closely, making the tea on automatic pilot. She tells the story in great detail, taking care to make him feel the buzz in the Dartmouth café that day, and to smell the wet wool and french fries. He almost feels he can see and hear Jason. And then her story opens up, like she's been deliberately leading him down this corridor of description in order to bring him to this vista.

Harry stops with a teabag in mid-air and looks at her, eyes shining. Michael was talking of *you*, he repeats.

Lindsay nods, her eyes wide with wonder. Then she looks away, blinking quickly. I still can't believe I went there, she laughs. She rubs the corner of one eye, taking care not to mess her mascara, then lets both hands fall limp in her lap. I'm the one who keeps telling my dad there aren't any answers to this, she says. But at the first hint of an explanation I drive two hours in a blizzard to confront a total stranger with this off-the-wall idea. She looks at Harry and tosses her hands in the air in a helpless gesture.

Well, I think you should be proud of yourself.

Proud of myself? *Why?*

Well, he says, it's one thing to come up with a theory like that, but it's another to call the guy and drive up to see him and ask him flat-out. I wouldn't have had the *chuzpah* to do it. But look what you got for yourself, just by having the balls to go looking. He pours her cup of tea.

Well, she says, confounding the tea with milk and sugar. If there *was* an explanation I had to know what it was. You know? I couldn't just let it go. She stirs the tea, sets down the spoon. So I guess I'm glad I went. She lifts the cup to her lips and blows, then takes a tentative sip.

I'm sort of glad I was wrong though, she muses, warming her hands on the cup. In a way I didn't want my brother reduced to a puzzle piece, you know? I didn't want him summed up that way. I mean, I wanted to understand, I did. But there was this little sliver of me that didn't really want to reduce his life, and his death, to a simple equation. You know what I mean?

Harry nods.

She stares at him a moment, lingering with that thought, then sets her teacup down. So, she says. What are we doing today?

Oh, he says. Just some finishing touches. Little details, tiny perfections. I'm just being fussy, really. At this point, it's really more about disengaging from the painting than it is about finishing it.

He slices a lemon in half, then quarters.

It's like I'm backing out of a room, he says, painting the floor around me until I finally reach the threshold. Then I step out and paint right up to the sill and finally I'm out of the picture for good. He squeezes some lemon into his tea, and smiles. Shall we get started?

She nods, and together they move to the studio. Harry busies himself with the music while Lindsay takes her place in the chair by the table, then he moves across to the easel as the music begins, shaking his arms out, sighing deeply. He settles himself on his stool and looks at her, then he looks at the painting, then he looks at her again.

Lift your chin a little? he says. She complies. A little to the left? She turns her head a bit. He studies her, then studies the painting, then her, then the painting again, and finally he makes a mark on the canvas.

As he works, he asks her all his questions about her parents, about her finals, about Christmas, he wants to know everything. But this isn't as easy as making tea, he can't really work on auto pilot, so eventually they do slide into an easy, extended silence, and let the music carry them. In time, it begins to snow outside.

So what are you going to do next? says Lindsay at last. Once this painting is done?

He doesn't answer right away, lost in a deepening shadow. I don't know, he murmurs finally. I've got a commission lined up in the spring, but I can't get started until the woman returns from Florida.... He frowns at the canvas, recoils from it, glances at her, then makes a mark. Until then, though? he says. I don't know.

He steps back from the easel to study the canvas, then sets down his brush. What I *should* do, he says, wiping his hands on a rag, is go out and find new people to paint. Just go find people on the street, and approach them, the way I approached that telephone lineman up there by the door. He perches on the edge of his stool and takes a sip of tea. But I'm afraid I might end up going back to that same old painting of Eric.

Lindsay looks over at the painting hanging behind the couch. I thought it was finished, she says.

Harry sighs and shakes his head.

What's the matter with it?

He shrugs. I'm not satisfied with it.

Why?

Because it's not him, I guess. He gazes at the painting, thinking. I guess it's just that simple. He glances at Lindsay. Because it's not him. He laughs at himself. Pretty obvious, isn't it? Doesn't matter how many paintings I paint, it's never going to be him. But I can't seem to get it through my head. I mean, I know it's true. But knowing something here—he points to his head—isn't the same as knowing something here, you know? He taps his chest with his fist, then gazes back at the picture. Maybe I should just paint him out, he muses, the way I did with Michael. Just make it a painting of an open door.

Lindsay considers the painting. Maybe you shouldn't try to have a painting of Eric at all, she says. Maybe you should just keep an image of him in your mind, or something. Or.... Well you've got photos of him, right?

Yeah, I've got a few.

Well, maybe for you, for a painter, a photograph is better. It kind of gets you out of the picture. You can't look at it and blame yourself for not getting it right. No matter how good the painting is, you'll always have that reaction, that you didn't get it right. And we both know that looking at Eric and blaming yourself for not getting it right…. We both know what that's about.

Harry laughs and nods, then sighs and looks back to his easel. There is Lindsay, vibrant and alive. Michael, dreamy and removed. Shadows, colors, textures, shapes. The smell of paints and linseed oil. A world that no longer needs him. He sets down his mug and stares at the canvas. Well, he says quietly. This is done.

She glances at him, surprised. Can I see?

He steps back and she comes to stand next to him. He is aware of how close she is, aware of her faint scent even in this smelly corner.

Yeah, she says. That's lovely. That's really lovely, Harry. I think you did the right thing, changing it. It would have been easy for you just to give my mother what she wanted, or what she thought she wanted, then take the money and run. But this has much more truth in it. She turns to him and smiles. I really admire how hard you struggled to find a way to do that.

He tips forward in a slight bow.

She turns back to the painting, lets her weight settle on one hip. Every time I look at this, she murmurs, I'll remember what Jason said. She glances at Harry. I don't even know if he was telling the truth; it might have been something he just made up to make me feel better. She looks back at the canvas. But it was a lovely thought.

She stares at the painting, drifting in thought, then lets out a long deep sigh. Maybe we're just not asking the right questions, she says, exasperated. *Why did Michael shoot himself? Why did Eric jump off the roof? Why didn't they come to us?* She lifts her arms, lets them slap to her sides. Maybe we're not supposed to know. Maybe what they did to themselves.... She turns and crosses to the window, looking out at the snow. Maybe that was just private, she says. Maybe when someone does that, it's just between them and God, you know? She turns and looks back at Harry. Maybe that's where we have to get to with this, just let it be between them and God.

I don't think much about God, says Harry.

I don't either, says Lindsay. Maybe we should.

Harry watches her intently.

I mean, maybe what Michael and Eric did, maybe it was an act of great faith, you know? It's possible, isn't it? Maybe their faith that God would take care of them was just so great that they dared deliver themselves into His hands. Maybe what they did was make a pact with God.

That sounds like a dangerous thought.

Why?

If everybody thought that way....

She turns back to the window. I don't care what everybody thinks. I'm just trying to find a way to live with what Michael did to himself. She stares out at the snow a moment longer, then looks at her watch. Well, she says. I have an appointment.

With whom? says Harry, a little hurt.

She turns around with theatrical flourish. Rudy the Marvelous, my acting teacher. He has hair the color of mustard. She picks up her teacup and takes it to the kitchen, then moves back out to the studio and pulls on her coat, slinging her pack onto her shoulder. She takes a look around the room. I'll miss this place, she says.

Drop by anytime, says Harry. You're just around the corner.

Yeah, she says. Maybe I will. She looks around the room again, then lets her gaze travel to the painting of her and her brother on the easel. See you, Michael, she murmurs. She lingers a moment, almost as if she's waiting for him to answer, then she turns and heads up the stairs.

Harry follows her up and when she stops on the balcony to take yet another look around, he draws up next to her and gazes across the room with her. It feels to him as if they are standing at the rail of a ship, looking at the land fall away after a journey abroad, thinking of all they've experienced there and all they're leaving behind.

Do you think you'll fall in love again, Harry?

Hmm, he murmurs. Hope so.

Yeah, she says. Me too. She gives him a sad and hopeful smile, then turns and walks out the door.

At the lift she turns to consider him, a little sheepishly. I want to thank you, she says, for putting up with my attitude in those early meetings. I can't believe I was such a bitch.

Neither could I, Harry laughs.

Their laughter trails off, and they look at each other awkwardly. Then they both start to speak at once. Harry laughs. Go ahead.

No, you go ahead.

No, you.

I was just going to say, says Lindsay. She shrugs. I'm going to miss you.

That's what I was going to say.

She looks at him, eyes glittering, then draws him to her and kisses his cheek. She is soft and young and fragrant and catches Harry completely off-guard. You are a very nice man, Harry Garrett, she says. Thank you for calling me *valiant*.

The lift arrives and she opens the door, then turns back to him. Find a little comfort, Harry. Find yourself a little love. She kisses him again quickly. Then she wraps herself in her coat, enters the lift and closes the gate.

Hey Lindsay? he says. She looks up at him. He lifts his fist beside his shoulder in the gesture of solidarity. Pray for the dead, he says to her. And fight like hell for the living.

She settles into herself and fixes her gaze on him, giving him a private smile. Good luck Harry, she murmurs.

31

David pauses at the door to the study, watching Marjorie at work. Her face is lit from below by the pool of light from the lamp beside her, the white plane of her holiday letter reflected in her glasses. She folds the letter precisely in half, then in half again, folds it inside the Christmas card, then slides the card in the envelope, setting it aside to be sealed and stamped later. She draws another copy from the pile and begins the process all over again.

David has seen the letter she's sending. He read it at the dinner table a couple of nights ago while his dinner got cold in front of him. *We lost Michael last year,* it said. *He took his own life. We don't know why.*

David looked up at her, surprised. Are you sure you want to say this?

There are people who don't know, she said. The Chases, the Holts. Dan Derrington. People ought to know.

But...said David. No hunting accident?

She shook her head, lips pursed, eyes down.

He considered her a moment, wondering what had changed her mind, but resisted the temptation to ask. It wasn't a time for opening up discussion. He pushed the paper back toward her. OK, he said. If that's what you want.

He watches her now as she signs another letter and folds it into the card, matching the corners perfectly, rubbing her nail three times across each crease, as if she were executing some precise and important ritual.

I'm ready, he says softly, so as not to startle her.

She glances up, startled anyway. OK, she says. I'll be right there.

He watches her a moment more, then turns back to the living room, assessing once again the big blue spruce in the bay window to be sure he's set it up straight and gotten the lights distributed evenly.

Are you sure, says Marjorie, joining him, we shouldn't wait for Lindsay?

He shakes his head; he has thought this through. I want her to walk into the house and have it just waiting for her, like a gift. I want this to be a good Christmas for her. Before, you know, I go.

Marjorie nods. Let's do it, then.

David picks up the box of ornaments and sets it on the coffee table, then stands there a moment looking at it, at the word XMAS hand-lettered on its side.

Seems like it ought to say PANDORA, doesn't it? he says. He glances at Marjorie, gives her a rueful smile.

Come on, she says. I'll help.

She crosses the room, lifts the top off the box. And there they all are, like the gifts of the Wise Men, all the familiar ornaments sparkling in the light—the glass baubles, the sled, the Santas, the reindeer, the crystal drops from old chandeliers, the snowflakes Lindsay and Michael made in elementary school.

I think we need a drink, says David.

He ducks into the kitchen and quickly returns with a bottle of scotch and a glass for each of them. He pours them both two fingers, then hands a glass to her and they each take a sip, staring at the ornaments as if at any moment they might start moving.

Well, says David at last. Let's get started.

It is heavy lifting, trimming this tree, remembering all the years before. The year when they stayed up late to assemble Michael's electric train set so the kids would find it running beneath the tree, like in all the old illustrations. The year of the sled, the baseball mitt. The year of Lindsay's new piano.

Do you remember the year? says Marjorie, kneeling by the tree to adjust a low-hanging garland. That little garden gnome, remember? That we had out on the terrace?

David watches the memory surface in his mind.

Back in Dayton, she says. You suspended it from the upstairs window so it danced in front of the living room window.

He stops to sip his drink, and nods.

She sits back on her heels and re-enacts the moment. I told the kids, *Oh look, Santa's elf! Checking to see if you're in bed! Santa must be on his way!* And they *ran* over to the window....

David closes his eyes and smiles, rocking on his heels. He has to concentrate to keep his balance.

Then you yanked on the wire to make the thing fly away, but the wire broke and the thing fell *splat* in the garden....

David laughs silently, eyes still closed, and they drift a moment, each of them privately faltering over the memory.

We had some good times, didn't we? says Marjorie.

Some of the best, says David.

He feels the weight now in his chest, the by now familiar sensation of the air being slowly pushed out of him, as if he is being crushed beneath a rock, his bones pressed to the breaking point. This is the moment he fears most of all, this is the moment he needs to avoid before it crushes him into extinction. He collapses into a chair and covers his face with his hands, listening in the dark to the horrible sounds that are coming out of him.

He feels Marjorie's hand on his neck, feels her arm across his shoulders, feels the nearness and warmth of her, then he turns and buries his face in her neck. She holds him and rocks him and murmurs to him until he is quieted.

I'm sorry, he says, sitting up and wiping his eyes on his sleeve.

Marjorie's hand is still resting on his back. She reaches up to stroke his hair. It's the resistance that hurts, isn't it? she says. Even more than the pain itself.

He turns to look at her. She meets his gaze without expectation. He's not sure she's ever looked at him quite like this before. It's as if he had entered into a secret room and found her standing there, her gaze is as simple as a statement of fact, as open as a door, ajar.

32

Lindsay takes a moment for herself before she knocks on the door. It's the same sort of moment she's learned to take before she steps onto a stage, or begins a scene in class —a moment to breathe, to collect herself and focus her intention. It's a satisfying thing to do, like clasping hands with a friend in agreement. Her favorite moment in theater always used to be the applause, but lately she's come to think of this moment of self-communion as the peak.

She squares her shoulders, takes a deep breath and knocks on Rudy's doorjamb. He turns and motions her in. It is a most amazing office —an Oriental rug on the floor, dark green walls hung with theater posters, an easy chair with a floor lamp beside it with a fringed Victorian shade —it looks like a South End drawing room. Rudy is seated at his desk, his mustard-colored hair seeming to glow in the shaft of sun from the window. Lindsay has to choose between the easy chair by the lamp and the straight-back chair by the window. She chooses the straight-back chair. She doesn't know what this meeting is for, but she wants to be alert, and she wants her head as high as his.

Forgive me, he says, as he turns away to finish off a scone. I missed my lunch earlier and I was absolutely starving. He dusts his fingers over the paper bag, then crumples it into a ball and plunges it into the wastebasket. So, he says, turning to her again. How are you today?

OK, she says. I'm fine.

He looks at her a moment as if he is assessing her. Good, he says at last. Good. He sits back in his chair and glances around his office. I've been... He clears his throat. The reason I called you in... He looks at her. I've been impressed with the work you've been doing lately in class. I think you've come a long way in a very short time.

Lindsay squares herself. Thank you. She grins. Must be the good instruction.

Yes, he smiles. I expect so. He glances out the window. That piece you did the other day, that scene from *The Seagull?*

Yes.

He looks back at her. That was very good.

Thank you. Yeah, I worked hard on that. It was a real stretch for me.

I know. That is a very hard speech. I don't assign it to everyone. In fact, some of my colleagues were appalled that I gave it to you, given what happened with your brother last year. They thought that maybe I should give you only comedy, certainly not a play that has a suicide at the end. But I had a hunch about you. I wanted to see what you'd do with it.

Well, she laughs. It was a challenge.

It is. He nods. A challenge. He squints at her. There was a moment... He leans in closer. There was a moment when you turned away from us and this, this *sound* came out of you. He chews on his lip. What was that?

Oh, says Lindsay, blushing. I don't know. That just happened one night in rehearsal, so I left it in. I liked it.

He nods, still squinting at her.

I sort of came to think of it, she says shyly, as the sound of her heart creaking open.

Rudy's eyes widen. Huh, he says. He scoots his chair closer. And there was another moment, he says, when you suddenly *laughed.* It was totally unexpected. What happened there?

Oh that, she says. It *was* unexpected. I was just getting so distracted by all the noise, you know? The people in the hall, the traffic outside, Andy's coughing. It seemed funny to me and I just decided to stop fighting it. Instead of trying to block it all out, I just let it in.

And how did that feel?

Well, she says. She hadn't really thought about how it felt. It was kind of weird. The words were taking care of themselves. The words were all automatic, like I was singing a song I knew really well. And what was more important was…I guess it was the presence of all those other people. I felt like I was myself and all of them too, or something. I don't know. I sort of felt like I was *all* of the people in that room, *all* of them doing that speech. Like I was funneling the Nina part of every person in the room.

Yes? he says.

Well, yeah. I guess I sort of felt like I was *encompassing* the room, instead of trying to fill it up. Like the room was a part of me, instead of the other way around. I don't know…

Rudy sits back and observes her as if she is an object, some kind of urn in a museum. What are your plans after graduation?

Oh, she exhales. I don't really know. I'd always thought I'd go down to New York and just see what happens. Audition for everything, like everyone else. But lately…? I don't really know.

Have you thought about graduate school?

Graduate school? *Me?*

There are some good schools around. Some of them offer very good training. Yale. NYU. The Old Globe in San Diego.

But those are drama schools.

Yes.

I'm in musical theater.

Yes, he says. I know. Lindsay can hear the taint of disdain in his voice. He glances out the window. He seems to be searching for something. I'd like to see you get some more training in drama, he says. If you want to. I think once you started exploring it further, you might find simply acting more and more compelling. I like NYU in particular because they train actors as an ensemble. It's a wonderful way to develop your art.

My art?

He shrugs. Acting is an art.

I never really thought of myself as an artist before. I'm more of a gypsy, a song-and-dance kind of girl.

He shrugs again. You've grown. Or maybe you've just discovered a deeper place in yourself, to draw on.

Lindsay doesn't respond.

Look, he says. I know what a struggle this last year has been for you. We're all… Of course. This is a small school.

Lindsay nods.

Sometimes experiences like that… He sucks his breath through his teeth. Sometimes experiences like that, as horrible as they are…they carve a deeper place in us. Like a river, carving a gorge through rock. And sometimes, if we're lucky, we have a choice what to fill that gorge with.

He rocks back in his chair, lets his feet dangle above the floor, and considers her. Maybe this is what you can do, he says. With this awful card that life dealt you.

He watches her. She doesn't respond.

He leans forward, elbows on knees, like a coach. Maybe you can *use* it, he whispers. Maybe spin it into gold. He gazes up into her eyes. Maybe you can carry it like a torch to light the world around you, to light the way for others. Maybe wear it emblazoned across your chest. Your humanity.

Lindsay stares at him, transfixed.

Rudy rolls his eyes and wags his head. I'm a theater person, he says, sitting back. He looks out the window and laughs. One might even say a Drama Queen, mightn't one? Then he looks back at her. But you get what I mean. Do you not?

If life hands you a lemon, she says, make lemonade.

Well, says Rudy. I daresay that I rather prefer my rendition. But lemonade, yes. If you must. He tweaks his mustache. Look. Here's what I propose. If you're interested, I'll work with you to prepare an audition for graduate school. We can work on that speech from *The Seagull*. You've got a good purchase on it, but we could make it even better. It is a great audition piece —that's one of the reasons I assigned it to you. Let me work with you on it. Then go audition at NYU. I'll write you a letter of recommendation, I'm sure you can get others. And let's see what happens. What do you say?

Lindsay swallows twice. I don't quite know what to say. I never thought about this before.

Well, says Rudy. Will you give it some thought? I think it would be worth your while.

Is it expensive?

It isn't cheap. And of course living in New York…

I'd have to talk to my parents.

Of course. And there are scholarships.

Scholarships?

You never know. But you may as well give it a shot. You're not sure what you want to do next. Maybe this would be the thing. Rudy glances at his watch. Well, he says. Whatever. I've got an important conference call coming up. He stands. Lindsay stands. Give it some thought, he says again, moving her toward the door. I'd love to work with you on it. Now if you'll excuse me… He pats his pockets. Where did I put…?

Oh Christ. He looks up at her, flashes a phony stage smile. Thanks for coming in, he says, and then he ducks back into his office.

Lindsay stands in the outer office as if she is in someone else's skin. She looks at Rudy's assistant, who is busy on the phone. She looks into the other office: vacant. She feels sort of like a lawn ornament, standing in the middle of this room for no particular reason, but she doesn't know quite where to move. A part of her wants to just stay in this moment, even though it's already over. A part of her, oddly, wants to call Harry.

She glances at Rudy's assistant again, then hugs her books to her chest and walks slowly out into the hall and to the top of the stairs. She pauses there for a moment, dizzy, as if she's perched on the edge of a cliff, as if she might fall, or as if she might fly. She feels the presence of someone behind her and turns, alarmed, but no one is there.

33

Harry turns at the hospital and shifts into second to climb the hill. It feels a little momentous to him, turning onto this street. He hasn't been here for three years and it's strange to be here now, alone. But he's spent so much of his life in waiting that he doesn't want to give himself the opportunity this time: he wants to go, to move, to act before he has second thoughts.

He crests the first hill then shifts into third and slows to search out the house. Will his memory serve him? All these houses look so much alike, built all at once in the '50s and '60s, but he finds the house without much trouble. He pulls on the brake and jumps out of the van, and by the time he gets to the door Mary Stiles has opened it wide. Harry! she says. Hello! Come in!

Mary, he says. How have you been?

Oh, I can't complain, she laughs. I do, of course. You know me. I've always got a complaint in me, but no one ever wants to listen. Come in, come in, she says, stepping back to make room for him. Would you like some coffee? Let me get you some coffee cake, she says, leading him into the kitchen.

He follows her through the dining room with its far-too-big table and breakfront and surveys the once-familiar kitchen. Lots of snapshots and kiddie drawings on the refrigerator. Frilly curtains at the window. An old clock radio on the yellow formica kitchen table. The coffee cake is set out, still in its wrapper, next to two plates and napkins.

Here we go, she says, handing him a coffee mug. She picks up the plates and napkins. And if you'll get that…. She nods to the coffee cake. Let's go into the living room.

The living room is small and dim and so crowded it almost looks like a furniture showroom. There are doilies on the tables and chair arms, framed photographs on the tabletops, an enormous television.

Harry sits and looks at her. She looks the same, maybe a little more harried. Her hair is wilder than it was, but it's still the same faded red—a difficult color, Harry thinks, to get right in a painting. Her face looks a little drawn, a little tired, pale and dry. But she has good bones, Mary always had good bones. He is glad to see her, at some level. In some ways, he always liked her. She seemed to have a good heart in her, if she'd just stop talking long enough to hear what it had to say.

It was such a pleasant surprise, she's saying now, to get your call! It's been so long since I've seen you. Have you been well? You're looking fit as a fiddle. Help yourself to the coffee cake. It's nothing special but I've always liked it. I've been eating this coffee cake for years, for *years*. So much has happened since I last saw you. Ken and Carol have a new baby…

As she talks, Harry looks around at all the family photographs. Pictures of all the kids and their kids at their various stages. There's Susan, Eric's sister, the nurse. And Kevin, his younger brother, in his policeman's uniform. There's Eric at two or three sitting on a photographer's drape, probably at Sears or Bradlee's, beaming at the camera. All pudgy and awkward and very red-haired, wearing a dopey striped shirt. The color is very faded. And there he is in his high school yearbook photo, looking ridiculously earnest and tidy, not the Eric Harry knew at all. Gazing off into the distance as if he has his eyes trained dreamily on his glorious future, and wearing a tennis sweater. A tennis sweater!

Well anyway, says Mary. Where was I? Oh, Susan! She's still working at Children's Hospital. She's doing very well, but I think she works too hard. I try to get her to slow down but she never listens to me. Nobody ever listens to me...

It's like music to her, thinks Harry. Like singing. It doesn't seem to matter what she's talking about, it's the making of sounds that matters to her, it's her way of establishing herself in the world. Harry always imagined she talked aloud when she was alone, just to know that she was there, but Eric said it wasn't so. *She needs an audience,* he said. *Good Christ, that woman needs an audience.*

So Harry is her audience while she rambles on about her children and their children, as if Harry will be interested as a matter of course. And he is, in a mild sense. But hearing their names again, hearing the soap opera updates on their lives, is depressing in a small way. To think that their lives continue on, pretty much unchanged, as if Eric's death hadn't had any impact at all. He was here and then he wasn't, and their lives just continue on. They still keep pumping out their kids. Still keep working too many hours. Still keep screwing up their love lives. They're like some endless video loop, just doing the same things over and over, the same boring things again and again. How could they just go on like this?

So, he says at last, breaking into Mary's monologue. I've brought you something.

Huh?

I've brought you something I want you to have.

Oh? she says, surprised. How nice!

It's in the van. Can you wait just a minute?

Well of course, she says. My goodness! Exciting!

Harry goes out to his van and pulls the painting out of the back, all wrapped in brown paper and twine, and takes it into the house, leaning it against the fireplace.

What is this? says Mary.

This is a painting, says Harry. I did of Eric. I've been painting pictures of him for the last three years, trying to capture who he was. I've burned a lot of them. It's just been so hard...It's so hard to capture...You know.

But of course she doesn't know, he thinks. He stops talking and looks at her. She is watching him, wary, concerned. She seems unsure where he's going with this and unsure she wants to come along.

Anyway, he says. I don't know. I just...I just wanted you to have this. It isn't perfect, it isn't Eric. But it's the best I could do. Of all the paintings, this one comes closest. I don't think I can do better than this. And I just thought.... I just thought I'd like you to have it.

She stares him, her watery eyes glazed blue and urgent. She looks braced. And again, Harry has the impression of sturdiness from her. *I can take this,* she seems to be saying. *Go ahead. Hit me again.* But her gaze also seems to be saying, *I know you have to do this. I know you think this is an act of kindness, and maybe it will be.*

So, he says. Here it is. He unwraps the canvas. And there is Eric in the doorway, one foot in the room, one foot out.

Mary stares at it. She looks up at Harry with her watery eyes, then looks back at the painting. Harry moves around so he can look at it with her, and then she starts to weep. He sits next to her, puts his arm around her shoulder.

I'm sorry, she says. I'm sorry.

Don't be sorry.

I'm just.... It's just....

I know.

She gathers herself, with effort. It's a very good painting, isn't it? she says. His eyes, his hair. Those eyes. That really captures him, doesn't it?

Well, I did my best.

Oh, but it's very good. I can't really take this. It's too valuable.

No, he says. I want you to have it. You can put it in the attic, if you want. But I just thought.... I guess I thought it ought to be here, somehow. I don't know. It just.... I don't know. I want you to have it.

She looks at him. Then she leans back and seems to study him. It occurs to Harry that at some level she is just realizing he is here. How have you been doing? she says softly.

Oh, he says, surprised to be asked. OK, I guess. He shakes his head. Not so well, I guess. He looks at her, laughs a little laugh. It doesn't get any easier.

She studies him a long moment. No, she whispers. It never does.

She reaches up and strokes his cheek, smiling a wan smile, then looks back at the canvas.

He did have beautiful eyes, didn't he?

34

Lindsay is examining a telescope, a handsome brass and wood affair with a felt-lined box, wondering if it would make a good Christmas present for her father, when she looks up and sees them. A couple probably in their mid-twenties, looking at an oversized picture book together. They seem to be very straight—a camel's hair coat on him, long dark wool on her, both with very tidy hair. Not the sort of people she would ordinarily take interest in, except for the way his body leans in over hers. The closeness of their cheeks, as they turn the pages. They are discussing the book, apparently trying to decide if it would be a good gift for someone. The same sort of problem Lindsay is having—except they have each other to wonder with, instead of muttering to themselves like they've recently been deinstitutionalized.

Finally the girl closes the book and turns to the guy, smiling up at him, and he steps back to let her pass, turning to look one last time at the book as they head toward the door. Lindsay sets the telescope down and drifts out after them, as if she were caught in their wake. She follows them down the street a short way, watching the way the girl holds onto the guy's arm, the way he tilts his head toward her, to listen. She loves how relaxed they are together, how much they assume each other's affection. But then she feels ridiculous, like some sort of third-grade private eye spying on them, so she turns into Starbuck's.

It has been such a busy time, these last weeks, with the culmination of her classes and then the final exams, and on top of all that the Christmas shopping. She hasn't had time to think about much of anything other than plugging through to the end, when she can go home and relax.

She is eager to go home, this Christmas. She wants to see her old friends, she wants to sleep in her old bed. She wants to go to Michael's grave. And she wants to see how her parents are doing. She has called a couple of times but no one ever picks up, and when her mother has called back, Lindsay has never had her phone on. Her father hasn't called at all. She doesn't know what to make of that.

She sips her coffee and looks around the café. At the table next to her, a couple is warming their hands over their steaming coffees and gazing into each other's eyes. It occurs to Lindsay that the city has been invaded by lovers, that Cupid has cut a wide swath through town but somehow managed to miss her apartment. It makes her think of Aldo—his long eyelashes, the warmth of his touch, the lanky grace of his body—but she dismisses the thought at once.

She takes a deep breath and sits back, watching the people standing in line, watching the counter help call out their codes—*decaf, grande, latte, mocha*—watching the lovers coo. It is a rare moment's rest. And that, perhaps, is what has changed since the start of the semester. For the first time in a year, she feels that she can just rest for a moment. In the midst of all the Christmas rush, all the hurrying people and noise, she can rest. The shopping will get done, or not. Love will come in time, or not. Her brother's memory will fade.

Michael's memory will fade. Already she can't call his face to mind, or the sound of his voice. What comes to mind instead is the picture that Harry painted. It is a sadness to realize that when she thinks of him, that is what comes to mind, rather than Michael himself. It feels like somehow Michael has been taken away from her, and for a moment she feels a surge of righteous anger toward her mother for commissioning the thing. But then she sighs and sets it aside. Because of course Michael was taken from her long before that painting was made.

And then it comes over her once again. Michael's absence. Michael's pain. It sets off a tumult in her stomach, a churning that has been invading her at will for the past year. She's always tried to evade it before. She'd go to dance class or try to nap. Or, most urgently, call Aldo. But this time she just sits there and pays attention to it. She stares at her hands on the tabletop, at her nails. Her ring. She watches the way her fingers move, like little creatures exploring each other. The scratch on her knuckle, the freckle on her finger. She turns up her wrist, to look at it. She remembers the grid of scarlet, seeping, but now the skin is perfectly smooth, all healed, as if she had never cut herself at all.

It takes a long moment, then moments more, but the ache does dissipate, slowly. She knows it will be back, that it will always come back, then again. But she's gotten through it this time, so maybe she'll get through it next time too. Maybe just by watching her hands. Maybe just by concentrating on that place inside her, where everything gathers. She looks around the café at the people behind the counter, the customers standing in line, the lovers at the tables. She listens to the whoosh of steamed milk, notes the smell of wet wool. She takes a deep breath, and then another. Then she gathers up her bags and moves on.

35

On Friday, Harry takes the painting to a carpenter Gillian's dealer has recommended in the SoWa District. It feels odd to be driving it down there; he feels the way he imagines it feels to drive your child off to college—this sense of important leave-taking and inevitability, millions of things to say but nothing left to say at all. Whatever he could do has been done. It is no longer up to him.

It is a gray and moody morning, unusually mild for December. The traffic is outrageous, what with all the Christmas shoppers, and the famous Boston jaywalkers are even more brazen than usual, but Harry is in no hurry. He watches the day out his windshield as if he is watching *cinema verité*, feeling quite collected.

He finds the right address, an old brick industrial building, rings the bell and is buzzed in. When the carpenter opens his door on the second floor, Harry has a jolt of recognition. It isn't that he knows this guy—this Jeff, as he introduces himself—he's sure he's never seen him before. Surely he would remember all that funky, curly hair. But something about him feels—well, no, *familiar* is not the word, but Harry doesn't know what the right word is. When he shakes Jeff's hand, he feels a current in it.

Jeff pulls on a parka and leads Harry back down the stairs to the van, then helps him haul out the painting and slide it onto the freight elevator. As they ride back up, chatting aimlessly about the building—its original use, its conversion, the politics, who lives in it now—Harry notices Jeff has some acne scarring on his face that gives him a rugged quality, makes him look like he's been through something. Is that what seems familiar? he wonders. Or is *comfortable* the word?

They carry the painting into Jeff's shop and lean it against a table. Dr. Laura is on the radio. You actually listen to her? says Harry.

I like to hear what people are saying, Jeff says. It's educational. And besides, I think it's a good idea to keep track of the enemy. He changes the station to quiet jazz, then takes off his parka. Harry sees how his chest fills out his sweatshirt.

Aren't you warm? says Jeff. Take your coat off, have a seat. Want coffee?

Oh, says Harry. Oh, sure. Uh, yes.

Cream and sugar?

Just black.

Ah, says Jeff, handing him a mug. I guess you're from the Midwest.

Harry looks at him, amazed.

Jeff grins. I grew up in Indiana. I can recognize those flat Midwestern vowels at twenty paces.

Oh, says Harry. Oh. I thought…. He looks at his coffee. No, never mind.

Well, says Jeff. Let's have a look. He plants himself in front of the canvas, his coffee mug cupped in both hands. Nice, he says. That's very nice.

Harry wonders if he really thinks so. He imagines this guy prefers abstract, expressionistic work, or maybe funky left coast stuff. Edgy things. Downtown hip. Certainly not carefully rendered portraits, commercial trash. Harry can tell his compliment is actually condescending. Or is he just being paranoid?

Who are these people? says Jeff.

Harry tells him the story—he offers up the long version, to extend the conversation—and Jeff is impressed with how Harry solved the problem. I like the palette too, he says. He studies it a moment longer, moves closer in then backs away. You have good brush technique.

Harry notices the way Jeff moves, how comfortable he seems in his body. You seem to know what to look for, he says.

I went to the Museum School a couple of hundred years ago. He turns to Harry. I started doing carpentry to pay my student loans and it ended up taking over my life. I do a lot of crating for the galleries around town—started out doing it for my friends, you know—so I get to see a lot.

You do any painting now?

Naw, says Jeff. It's been years. It bothered me for a while, but then I stopped thinking of myself as a painter doing carpentry, and started concentrating on just doing better carpentry, and I've been happy as a clam ever since. He turns back to the painting. I still like looking at all the stuff, though.

Harry sips his coffee, wondering what's hanging from that silver chain around Jeff's neck. What sort of carpentry do you do?

Finish stuff, for the most part. Bookcases, cabinets, stuff like that. And I make some furniture. He shows Harry a table he's working on, a whimsical thing made of birch—tapered legs intersected at random heights by metal spheres, with a trapezoidal top, so oddly shaped and weighted it doesn't look like it ought to be able to stand. But in fact it's very sturdy, he says, wiggling it to demonstrate that it doesn't wiggle. He looks at it proudly, assessing. All this work, he muses, and it's just something to toss the mail on. He grins at Harry. I love rich people. What would we do without them?

Harry bobs his head in agreement. Send some my way, will you?

Well, says Jeff. Let's do it.

Harry watches as Jeff sets to work, wrapping the painting in brown paper, then wrapping it again with bubble wrap and taping it six ways to Sunday. He is aware of the smell of coffee and wood and glue and varnish, and the sound of the steam banging in the pipes and hissing out of the radiators. He is aware of the quiet jazz and of the windows steaming up. He is aware, especially, of Jeff's hands.

It occurs to him to propose to Jeff that he paint a picture of him, maybe a detail of his hands, maybe wrapped around a coffee mug. Or maybe—what's under that sweatshirt? He settles back into his chair. Maybe this time he *won't* try to turn this person into an object.

He cradles his coffee with both hands and watches quietly as Jeff constructs a crate around the painting, sealing it safely inside. It feels like watching a burial, Harry thinks, committing a dead thing to the ground. The radiator hisses and knocks. The saxophone on the radio moans.

When Jeff finishes the crate he drives in one extra nail with a flourish, for luck. Seems like it should have taken longer, says Harry, mocking his own melancholy. It took so long to paint it.

We could break down the crate and start over, Jeff shrugs. I haven't got anything going this morning.

Harry hums a small laugh. They finish off the coffee, then carry the crate to the elevator and load it back into the van. Harry closes the door and pulls out his wallet. I really appreciate your doing this on such short notice, he says. My regular guy is out of town, and the client wants it there by Christmas.

No problem at all, says Jeff, stuffing the bills into his pocket without counting them. I can usually work things in. Give me a call whenever.

Harry pulls out his keys, then stands there a moment, dumbly, as if he doesn't know what to do next. Well, he sighs at last. He pats the back of the van. Time to say good-bye to another one.

There'll be others, says Jeff. He removes his glove to shake Harry's hand. Nice to meet you.

They shake, and Harry gets that buzz again. Likewise, he says. The same.

Jeff doesn't turn to go. A few flakes of snow come to rest on his curls. You traveling for the holidays?

No, says Harry. I'm staying here.

Jeff nods. Well, he says quietly, smiling. Maybe I'll see you around.

Yeah, says Harry. Yeah, maybe.

Harry climbs into the van and pulls into the street, then makes his way up Berkeley to Storrow Drive and heads toward Watertown. The sky is luminescent pearl, a cloud cover smooth as plaster with a smeary glow of sun behind it, trying to make itself known. It casts a weird glow on the world, an odd weak winter light that feels as featureless as his life to him, a great flat canvas waiting for him to make a mark on it, waiting for him to begin again. But for all the bleakness, Harry feels a rising in his chest and a catch in his throat, a yearning, and he finds himself wondering, Does he dare hope? Isn't hope the thing that brings you down? Isn't hope the dangerous thing? He remembers reading somewhere that hope and fear are the same thing—both worries about the future—so to minimize fear you must minimize hope, just stay in the present moment. But what is life, he thinks, without hope?

The UPS store is crowded with people shipping Christmas presents and Harry becomes preoccupied with jockeying in line, filling out forms, saying good-bye to his painting. He imagines Michael in the crate, pictures him nestled in there smiling out through the bubble wrap. And it makes him think of the painting of Eric, leaning on Mary Stiles' hearth. Eric in the doorway, with his beautiful, inscrutable eyes.

He watches the crate get carried off, then folds the receipt into his pocket and squeezes his way past the crowds, back outside. He climbs into his van and starts the engine, concentrating on the way the key slides into the lock, on the sound of the heat rushing up from the heater, on the weight of his shoes on his feet. He looks up at the sky and sees that it has just brightened a little—one layer of clouds has just slid away so you can actually see the shape of the sun, now a hazy ball of fire instead of just a smear.

He tries to imagine Eric up there, drifting in and out of the clouds, tries to imagine him making some sort of pact with God to take care of him, but it's inconceivable. The cigarette burns on his hands and legs, his sudden disappearances—where's the evidence of faith in that? Harry hunches over the wheel, suddenly aware of how deeply he's huddled inside his coat. He heaves a sigh. Maybe now, he muses. Maybe now that there are no cigarettes, maybe now that there are no hands and legs. Maybe now Eric has managed to make the pact he couldn't make in life.

It's something to hope for at least, Harry thinks. And what is life, after all, without hope?

He settles back into his seat and stares at the dashboard a moment, feeling more spacious inside, like a billow that's just been expanded. He fills his lungs and empties them, lays back his head and stares at the roof, feeling, for the moment, complete.

This is a pretty good van, he thinks. It's got a few good years in it yet. He lowers his gaze to the steering wheel, grips it hard and gives it a spank. Then he shifts the van into gear and pulls to the edge of the parking lot to wait for a break in the traffic. He has a moment's thought of Lindsay, poised on that piano bench—*valiant*—and it makes him smile. Then he perches himself alert at the wheel, determined now to grab his next chance to slip back into the stream.

ACKNOWLEDGMENTS

First thanks go to my friend Louis Briel, the painter who actually lived this story, or a version of it; it was my admiration for the way he dealt with the challenge that prompted me to start this book.

Thanks then to the people who helped me turn the story into a novel with their thoughtful readings and good suggestions: Ben Brooks, Carol Flynn, Pat Harrison, Jean Hey and Steven Holt.

Big thanks to the Boston Conservatory for opening their doors to me so I could observe how actors learn, to April Guenther for suggesting the likely hangouts and musical tastes of a punky art school student, to my brother Bruce for the tour of Cincinnati's environs and to Jan Donley for the well-timed kick in the butt.

As always, thanks to Richard Parks for his abiding commitment and for having that drink with Sarah Self. Thanks to Sarah and to David Gersh for passing the story to Caroline Link and major thanks to Caroline for taking it the next step. I consider her commitment to this project a tremendous honor.

My gratitude to Robert Cort and Scarlett Lacey for helping Caroline's vision become a reality and to all three of them for welcoming this screen novice into their midst.

Finally, and continually, my thanks to Richard MacMillan, who stood by me through this whole bloody process, cheering and advising. Let's hope the next one is easier.

Made in the USA
Monee, IL
29 September 2024